NO BILE!

alphonse ALLAIS

NO BILE!

translated from the french by
DOUG SKINNER

BLACK SCAT BOOKS
2018

NO BILE!

by Alphonse Allais

Translated from the French, with an introduction,
illustrations & notes on the text by Doug Skinner

ISBN 13   978-0-9992622-9-0

Cover art & book design by Norman Conquest

ACKNOWLEDGEMENTS:

This collection was originally published in Paris by Flammarion in 1893 under the title *Pas de Bile!* Facing page: cover of the original edition.

A NOTE ON THE TYPOGRAPHY:

Story titles have been set in the lively Victorian display font *Tilson Initials*, crafted by The Walden Font Co. in Winchester, Massachusetts. The text is typeset in *Minion Pro*.

BLACK SCAT BOOKS

Sublime Art & Literature

BlackScatBooks.net *&* **BlackScatBooks.com**

LES AUTEURS GAIS

ALPHONSE ALLAIS

(ŒUVRES ANTHUMES)

Pas de Bile!

PARIS

LIBRAIRIE MARPON & FLAMMARION

E. FLAMMARION, SUCC^r

26, RUE RACINE, PRÈS L'ODÉON

CONTENTS

WHY BE BILIOUS?

READERS WHO HAVE DEVOURED my earlier translations of Alphonse Allais may already be familiar with his background. For new readers, or for older ones who skipped the prefaces to get to the good stuff, here are some pertinent points.

Allais was born October 20, 1854, in the small coastal town of Honfleur, in Normandy. He didn't speak until he was three, and then became an exceptionally mediocre student. Despite his later reputation as a practical joker, he was not given to boyhood pranks.

His father ran the local pharmacy, so adolescent Alfi was duly packed off to Paris, to learn the rudiments of mixing prescriptions. He neglected, one could even say unabashedly, his studies for wine, women, and journalism. Slim, blond, with an unfettered imagination masked by an impassive facade (he was often compared to an English schoolteacher), he promptly became popular among the bohemians in Montmartre. He mixed with such wild-eyed youth as the Barbus, the Hydropathes, and the Zutistes, and began writing jokes and squibs for various ephemeral papers.

When Rodolphe Salis opened the cabaret Le Chat Noir

in 1881, Allais became a fixture. Le Chat Noir attracted the young and unorthodox; it became famous for its shadow puppet plays, its roster of fine poets and singers, and for Salis's habits of insulting the customers and underpaying the performers.

Le Chat Noir also published a paper (what is a cabaret without a paper?); Allais wrote for it, and eventually became editor. He contributed short stories, both comic and serious, appreciations of colleagues, literary parodies, and topical commentary. Like many in his circle, he also wrote monologues for Coquelin Cadet, an actor from the Comédie-Française who made a specialty of comic recitations. Allais also had the audacity to swipe the byline of Francisque Sarcey, a celebrated middlebrow theater critic, turning him into an overstuffed buffoon rambling on about his impotence and constipation.

Allais began to become known. His monologues were published by Ollendorff, which also released a collection of his *Chat Noir* columns, *A se tordre* (*Double Over*) in 1891. The next year saw the appearance of a second volume of what he called his "anthumous works," *Vive la vie!* (*Long Live Life!*), again taken from his *Chat Noir* columns. He was now established as a humorist, and left *Le Chat Noir* in 1892 to join a new paper aimed at a wider audience. It was called simply *Le Journal*, and was published by an impresario fully as flamboyant as Salis, Fernand Xau. Xau had, among other things, become celebrated as an interviewer, and managed Buffalo Bill's tour of France. He had the idea of putting out a literary paper that cost only a sou, and gathered a fine group of writers. Allais's column was unambiguously headed *La vie drôle* ("The Funny Life"), and he diligently set about the grim business of earning laughs.

The new column was different in some ways from the old. He had less space ("my space is limited, ferociously," he often told his readers), and he toned down some of his bohemian bawdiness. He still made fun of Sarcey (everyone made fun of Sarcey), but no longer forged his byline.

For his third book, then, he was at a crossroads. He had already compiled two books from his *Chat Noir* work, and had been writing only a few months for *Le Journal*. Much of his earlier work for *Le Chat Noir* had been short stories that didn't quite fit his role as comedian, and most of the later pieces were written as Sarcey. A pseudo-Sarcey column in a Montmartre paper was no problem, but putting them in a book might have been legally problematic.

So, in addition to his published columns, Allais included the monologues published by Ollendorff, and wrote several short pieces to fill out the book. Curiously, two of these were devoted to plugging his colleagues: excerpts from the comic paper *The Scalp Hunter* and from the young poet Franc-Nohain. Of course, that also meant less work for him.

Humor is notoriously as evanescent as a mayfly (a funny

mayfly). Allais has continued to be read long past the usual expiration date largely because of his inventiveness. Unlike his contemporaries, he mostly avoided standard comic tropes, coming up with fresh forms and ideas. His interest in wordplay led to such inventions as the neo-alexandrine (in which the syllabic count is irregular, but averages to twelve) and the holorime (two verses in which every word is a homonym), and earned him from Oulipo the title of "Anticipatory Plagiarist." His scientific background inspired such mock inventions as the anti-filter (to boost the immune system) and the corpse-car (a hearse powered by burning the deceased), which led the Pataphysical College to dub him their "Patacessor." Among the glimmers of prescience you will find here are the unprepossessingly-entitled "Jokes," based on a frankly 'pataphysical distortion of perception; "Absinthes," an early example of the internal monologue; and "The Gentleman and the Hardware Clerk," which is apparently one of those shopkeeper sketches from Monty Python.

Six of the pieces here appeared in my earlier translations. Allais reworked the three Captain Cap stories for his book about that immortal adventurer; I lifted the three Coquelin Cadet monologues for a collection of Allais's plays. Since I wanted to keep Allais's original lineup, I didn't delete them, but did add six uncollected stories, drawn from François Caradec's edition of the complete works. Five are from the same period as *No Bile!*; the last is later, but seemed a fitting way to mark Allais's departure from *Le Chat Noir*. As usual, my notes in the back of the book provide the original publication dates and explain the topical references. Allais's fictional characters often have punny names; rather than anglicize them, I've noted their etymology. Now for the good stuff. And don't be bilious!

Doug Skinner
New Paltz, NY
May 2018

THE MISERABLE WRETCH AND THE GOOD GENIE

Once upon a time there was a miserable Wretch... the most unfortunate there could be in the matter of miserable Wretches.

Without break or respite, bad luck, frighteningly bad luck, had hounded him, such bad luck that you could not find three like it in this century, so fertile in bad luck.

. . . .

That morning, he collected his meager resources into the pockets of his vest.

The entire amount comprised a capital of 1 fr. 90 (one franc and ninety centimes).

That was life today. And tomorrow? Miserable Wretch!

So, having dabbed a little ink on the white seams of his frock coat, he went out, in the fallacious hope of *finding* work.

That frock coat, once black, had been gradually transformed by Time, the great colorist, into a green frock coat; and the miserable Wretch, in all candor, now called it "my green frock coat."

His hat, which had also been black, had turned red (apparent contradiction in the workings of Nature!).

The green frock coat and the red hat set each other off vividly.

Placed together complementarily, the green was greener, the red redder, and, in the eyes of many people, the poor Wretch appeared to be an eccentric chromomaniac.

. . . .

The miserable Wretch's entire day was spent in futile pursuits, in stairways ascended and descended a thousand times, in long waits in waiting rooms, in endless errands. And all without the slightest result.

Miserable Wretch!

To economize on time and money, he didn't eat!

(Don't pity him; he was used to it.)

At six o'clock, unable to go on, the miserable Wretch collapsed before a table in a saloon on the outer boulevards.

A fine tavern that he knew quite well, where for four sous one had the best absinthe in the neighborhood.

For four sous, to be able to *stick a little paradise under your skin,* as the late Scribe[1] said, what a joy for miserable Wretches!

Ours had barely moistened his lips with the beatifying liquid, when a stranger sat at a nearby table.

The newcomer, of an unearthly beauty, contemplated, with infinite benevolence, the miserable Wretch as the latter numbed his pain with little sips.

"You don't seem happy, miserable Wretch?" said the stranger, in a voice so sweet that it was like the music of angels.

"Oh no... not a lot!"

"I like you, miserable Wretch, and want to brighten your life. I am a good Genie. Speak... What do you need to be perfectly happy?"

"I would wish for only one thing, good Genie: to be assured of a hundred sous a day until the end of my existence."

"Truly, you are not a hard man to please, miserable Wretch! And your wish will be granted immediately."

. . . .

Assured of a hundred sous a day! The miserable Wretch beamed.

The good Genie continued.

"Only, because I have other things to do than to bring you a hundred sous every morning, and since I know the exact length of your life, I will give it to you... in one lump sum."

. . . .

In onc lump sum!

Can you see from here the face of the miserable Wretch?

In one lump sum!

Not only was he assured of a hundred sous a day, but from now on he would have it... in one lump sum!

. . . .

The good Genie finished his mental calculation.

"Here: this is your tally, miserable Wretch!"

And he counted out on the table 7 fr. 50 (seven francs and fifty centimes).

The miserable Wretch, in turn, calculated the length of time the sum represented.

A day and a half!

Only a day and a half to live! Miserable Wretch!

"Bah," he muttered, "I've seen worse!"

And, gaily pocketing his money, he set out to spend his 7 fr. 50 with chorus girls.

1. Was it really the late Scribe? (Publisher's note.)

JOKES

One of my friends is a Norwegian painter, whose name is Axelsen, and who is quite the funniest creature that the earth has ever borne.

(It was to this same Axelsen that occurred the unhappy adventure I recounted not long ago.

Axelsen had offered his fiancée a watercolor painted with seawater, which watercolor was, due to its composition, subject to the influence of the moon. One night, during a terrible equinoctial tidal wave, with strong winds, the watercolor overflowed its frame, and drowned the young woman in her bed.)

Although only recently arrived in Paris, Axelsen had inspired great affection among many.

I should add, to be accurate, that these benevolent sentiments emanate principally from the bartenders on the boulevard Rochouart, the wine sellers on the boulevard de Clichy, the saloon proprietors on the avenue Trudaine, and, to close this humble series, the gentleman-innkeeper on the rue Victor-Massé.

In short, my friend Axelsen is one of those characters about whom one whispers: "He's a lad who drinks."

Axelsen gets drunk, that's understood. But in every case, not with what you bought for him. So, leave the boy in peace; he never hurt you.

Axelsen drinks only one liquid a day, a single liquid, but at frighteningly short intervals, and in dosages that have nothing to do with homeopathic doctrine.

Some days, it's rum, nothing but rum.

Some days, it's amaro, nothing but amaro.

Some days, it's absinthe, nothing but absinthe.

It's very rare that it be Saint-Galmier mineral water. Really, quite rare!

Axelsen, another eccentricity, professes the most formal contempt for the true, for the lived, for the real.

"How ugly it all is," he says, "everything that happens! And how beautiful is everything that we dream. Men who tell the truth, the whole truth, and nothing but the truth, are only pigs in the mud. Don't you think?"

"Positively, that's what we think," we reply, to keep him quiet.

"If humanity were not such *chuckleheads*,[i] how much happier we would be! We would consider the real as null and void, and live in an eternal ambiance of dreams and jokes. Only… we'd have to pretend to believe it. Right?"

"Good Lord, obviously!"

Proceeding from this wise principle, Axelsen only says things that are beside life, inexistent, improbable, chimerical.

The finest compliment he can pay a man:

"Very nice, your friend, and very illusory!"

Yesterday morning, we found ourselves installed, a few others and I, in the sunshine on the terrace of a distillery (eighteenth arrondissement), when up came Axelsen, a disturbed Axelsen.

He collapsed, rather than sat, onto a nearby chair, and fell silent, which was even easier for him since he had not yet opened his mouth.

"Well, then, Axelsen!" we greeted him. "Is something wrong? You look like you harbor some great sorrow."

"As much sorrow as Bernhardt herself."

(It is only appropriate to remark that Axelsen pronounces his Os as As, a detail that explains all the savor of the joke.)

"Perhaps you didn't sleep well?"

"I slept like a top."

"Then what's wrong?"

"What's wrong, you ask? I have just witnessed a truly heartbreaking spectacle! Oh yes, heartbreaking, and how much so! Waiter!… A vulnerary!… That will make me feel better, a vulnerary."

The vulnerary was brought, and I can assure you that Axelsen didn't give it time to grow moldy.

"It's not bad, this vulnerary! Waiter!… Another vulnerary!"

"Well, then! And this heartbreaking spectacle?"

"Ah, my friends! Let's not talk about it. I feel great sobs arising in my throat. Waiter!… A vulnerary! There's nothing like a vulnerary to drive back the great sobs that arise in your throat!"

"Will you speak, man of the North?"

"Here it is: I have just witnessed the departure of the omnibus that goes from the place Pigalle to the Halle-aux-Vins. It's horrible! All those poor people crowded into that rolling box!… And all those other poor people, who, having only three sous, must perch precariously on the roof, exposed to all the intemperance of the season, to cold, wind, blizzards, and frost in winter, in summer to sunstroke and mosquitoes. Ah, those poor people! Waiter… a vulnerary!"

"Yes, it's very sad, and unworthy of our era of progress."

"And their poor relatives! The poor sorrowing relatives, twisting their arms in despair, and dousing the sidewalk with their tears. There were poor old folks, with one foot already in the grave, and little ones barely at the threshold of life. And they were all weeping, for would they ever again see those that were leaving them? Waiter!… A vulnerary!"

"Poor people!"

"It was especially when the omnibus moved off that it was truly upsetting. Handkerchiefs waved, and great sobs inflated the chests of all those lamentable folks. And no priest, my poor friends, for those who were leaving, no priest to pray for a benediction from the Almighty!"

"The fact is that the omnibus company could very well

assign a chaplain to each station. It's rich enough to afford this small sacrifice."

"Finally the vehicle left… One moment it seemed to merge with a large streetcar arriving from la Villette, then the two masses separated, and the little omnibus became visible again, not for long, alas! For, at the top of the Cirque Fernando, it veered starboard and disappeared in the rue des Martys. Waiter!… A vulnerary!"

"And the relatives?"

"The relatives? I lost sight of them!… I have every reason to believe that they took advantage of a momentary inattention on my part to drown themselves in the fountain in the place Pigalle. No doubt their bodies will be found in the nets of the Fontaine-Saint-Georges… Waiter!… A vulnerary!"

"Axelsen!" one of us said gravely. "I wouldn't dream for a single minute of casting any doubt on the story you just told. But are you absolutely sure that everything happened exactly as you said?"

"Horrors! Horrors! This man dares accuse me of fraud! I'm choking… Waiter!… A vulnerary!"

1. The word *chucklehead* was recently revealed to Axelsen by M. Jules Lemaître's column in *Débats*. On the strength of that young and intelligent critic's judgment, Axelsen now uses the word *chucklehead* in the best circles on the rue Lepic.

A NASTY JOKE

There was a gentleman who was very rich, but enormously bored. And so, to dispel his ennui, he indulged in a thousand jokes on his contemporaries, all in the worst taste, besides.

One morning, he arrives at the public square, where masons regularly gather, in search of work. He notices two who look a little stupid:

"Would you like to earn twenty francs apiece, today?"

"You bet, monsieur!"

"Very well! Listen."

It concerns a wall, to be built at once and very quickly, but in such a way that it be immediately dry, and, once completed, indestructible.

The two masons procure everything they need: stones, and a certain cement they know.

The rich gentleman loads them onto a car, and takes them to a building that is far, far away, a mere gunshot, if that, from the thunder of God.

They enter a room lit by two narrow lancet windows, sturdily barred, and which look out on an old courtyard, a well rather, which seems a congress of every rank weed from every flora.

One mason says:

"It's not much fun here."

But the rich gentleman shows them their job: a door to

be walled up. One louis up front, the other when the task is completed.

At the very moment they laid the last stone in place, night began to fall.

With their sleeves, the masons wipe the sweat from their brows, with the satisfaction of a "job well done."

But a sudden pallor blanches their faces. The door... that door they had walled up so very consciously (and unconsciously), that door is the only way out of the room!

. . . .

And even though the incident happened some time ago, the rich gentleman never passes that masonry without a hearty laugh.

GERMS

The ardent Achilles, as everyone knows, was fed, in his youth, on the marrow of lions. This regular diet infused him with a courage, of which, afterwards, he gave many a proof.

It was the first step in a theory of adaptation that only needed to go further: it went further.

The disturbing method developed by papa Brown-Séquard is merely one particular case in this order of ideas.

The average man, fed daily on tiger or panther meat, soon becomes the cruelest of beings.

Treat yourself frequently to aged pork, and I will give you just twenty minutes to show all the exterior signs of senile swinishness.

A soldier who indulged willingly in the consumption of hares' hearts would soon become unfit to handle weapons, but if he also ate the feet (of the hares, not the weapons), he could be used for the rapid delivery of messages.

I could multiply the examples to infinity; it wouldn't be dirty, but would take up space, which is limited to me, ferociously.

No rule without its exception, however.

For example, myself:

If you want to please me, when invited to your house, just serve me a pretty grilled mackerel. Well, I cannot recall, on any pretext, having ever accepted a single sou from a woman!

All this preamble to tell you the story of these people, quite peaceful until now…

Having arrived unannounced at the house of a rural friend, they gathered at the table, informally, before an improvised omelet (by a newly-arrived maid, note this detail) and other dishes whose enumeration would only lengthen this story (and I said above that my space is limited, ferociously).

These fine people had no sooner consumed the omelet, when the host's crystal and other movable objects flew through space, hurled violently, for no apparent reason, by the guests.

These last did not stop at that… But the story of the ensuing violence… (As I said above…)

All that had happened was that the maid (newly arrived) had made the omelet using eggs from a henhouse especially patronized by fighting cocks, prized in all the contests in England and Flanders.

It's bizarre, all the same, to think that, in one of those eggs, in the tranquil yolk, in the untroublesome white, simmer the germs of violence, of hostility, of murder.

Nature is funny!

A HISTORICAL FOOT-NOTE

Many people were astonished, and with good reason, to see my name missing from the list of the new cabinet.

Should we see in this absence merely an unpardonable oversight, or was there indeed a formal decision to distance me from affairs?

The first hypothesis must be rejected. As for the second, France is here to judge.

On Monday, December 5, 1892, in the morning, at nine o'clock sharp, M. Bourgeois rang at my door. In the time it took to pull on my pants, and to pin my Academy officer ribbon to my flannel nightshirt, I went to him.

"M. Carnot has asked for you," he told me. "I have my car below. Are you ready?"

"A brief toilette and I'm off."

"Not necessary, you're fine as you are."

"But, my dear M. Bourgeois, you can't possibly think..."

M. Bourgeois didn't let me finish. With a vigorous hand, he seized me, rushed me down the four stories from my bachelor's ground-floor lodgings, and shoved me into his Berlin.

Five minutes later, we were at the Elysée.

M. Carnot received me the most graciously in the world; paying no attention to my elk-skin slippers, to my unceremonious jacket, nor to my balmoral (a sort of Scottish hat), the President showed me to a chair.

"What portfolio is particularly appealing to you?" he asked.

For a moment, I thought of the fine arts, because of the little students in the Conservatory, for whom the title of minister provides an excellent introduction.

I also thought of finance, because of what you might guess.

But patriotism spoke more loudly within me than licentiousness and cupidity.

In a firm voice, I replied:

"I ask to be entrusted, monsieur, with the ministry of war."

"Do you have in mind any reforms that you would propose, relative to this question?"

"And how!" I replied, perhaps a bit rudely.

With perfect good grace, M. Carnot invited me to explain.

"All right: I begin by abolishing the artillery…"

"!!!!!"

"Yes, because of the truly intolerable racket the cannons make when they're fired, a very annoying racket for those people whose homes are near the polygons."

M. Carnot made a slight gesture whose meaning I could not quite understand. I continued:

"As for the cavalry, its immediate disappearance also figures in my plans for reform."

"!!!!!"

"We would avoid, in this way, all those bruises on the buttocks, and all those falls from horses, that are the dishonor of standing armies."

"And the infantry?"

"The infantry? It would be lunatic and criminal to keep it! Have you ever served, monsieur, as a second-class foot soldier?"

For a few moments, M. Carnot seemed to collect his memories.

"Never!" he answered at last, decisively.

"Then you cannot know how the poor soldiers suffer, subject to blisters, to foot wounds, during those forced marches. You have no idea, monsieur, you have no idea!"

"And the engineers?"

"I have no particular prejudice against that special arm, but… Let me tell you: I had, a few years ago, a little girlfriend, as sweet as a rose, who was named Eugenia, but whom I called, in private, Engineer. One day, that young woman left me to go find a certain Caran-d'Ache, who later… But enough!… I felt deeply distressed by this abandonment, and still to this day, the mere mention of those three syllables Engin-eer reopens the scars of love on my heart…"

I paused; M. Carnot wiped away a furtive tear.

"We come to the bridge builders," I continued. "You, who are a serious man, monsieur, I am frankly astonished that you have kept until now, in the French army, individuals whose sole mission consists of making false teeth."

At this moment, the chief executive of our Republic arose, seeming to indicate that the interview had lasted long enough.

During all that time, we had had nothing to drink: I invited MM. Carnot and Bourgeois to go, with me, to have a vermouth at the wine seller's on the place Beauveau.

The gentlemen did not accept.

I saw no reason to insist; I retired with a polite salute.

THE FUTILITY OF IDIOT

Logic leads to everything, as long as it leads out again, as a wise man said.

That wise man was right; and the Pasteur who will discover, to kill it, the bacillus of the corollary and the microbe of the converse will perform quite a service for humanity.

Without going any further, I myself have a friend who would be the happiest boy in creation, but for the rage he has of drawing conclusions from facts, and arranging his life "logically," as he puts it.

Therefore, his existence is nothing but a forest of gaffes.

One little anecdote, among others, comes to mind:

At that time, he was a student, and not very rich. His monthly allowance served the purpose of buying drinks for all the little ladies who passed along the boulevard Saint-Michel. Therefore, his tailor received, every century or so, only derisory payments.

One fine day, impatient, this tradesman went up to the young man's room and "bangbangbanged" on his door.

Guessing what it was about, the young man breathed not a word, and even, following the ostrichian procedure, buried his head betwixt the bedclothes.

"Bang, bang, bang!" insisted the tailor.

Similar mutism.

Finally, the man lost his patience:

"Answer me, for pity's sake!" he cried. "I can see very well that you're here, because you left your boots by the door!"

The lesson did not go unheeded, and from then on, at dawn, my friend brought in his shoes.

Several days later, the tailor returned. His "bangbangbang" remained without reply. And since he insisted so noisily, it was my friend's turn to become angry. He cried, from his bed:

"Will you stop all that complaining in the hallway, you imbecile?… You can see very well that I'm not here, because my shoes aren't by the door."

A clumsy deception that made scant impression on the tradesman.

THE INTERMEDIARY

One could never risk before him a single "Well, I'm going to buy a pair of gloves," without him immediately intervening with "Would you like the address of a good glove maker?"

It was the same for shoes, with the difference that it was a good bootmaker that he offered.

And besides, it was the same for everything: for corks, safes, threshing machines, mummies, smoke absorbers, freight elevators, adult crocodiles, in a word for all those innumerable and multiform objects whose acquisition or sale constitutes what M. Pierre Delcourt calls "commercial transactions."

Had an uncouth little boy told him he wanted "nuttin," he would have immediately directed the child to an excellent supplier of almonds and filberts.

What could this eternal and unceasing solicitude have brought him? Oh! What little profits he must have made!

For my poor friend did not appear very rich. And often I too had the idea, at the sight of his appalling linen, to give him the address of a good shirtmaker.

Although these things do not concern us, neither you nor me, let me tell you that he was unable to pay his

October rent.

Nor had he settled for July, nor—poor fellow!—for April.

Furious, the concierge no longer brought him his mail, which consisted, besides, of nothing but prospectuses, circulars, clandestine periodicals, etc.

The landlord became involved, and threatened him with eviction.

And my poor friend could only reply:

"Would you like the address of a good process server?"

MODERN IDYLL

He lived on the mezzanine

She lived on the sixth floor.

He was a young man of about twenty-five, not an ugly boy, but as stupid as anything.

She was a young woman of about twenty-two, rather pretty, but a bit humorous.

His parents were retired shopkeepers, rich, bare owners, usufructuaries, and not such bad people, all the same.

Her father (for her mother was dead) was the retired head of a corps of engineers.

(Have you ever noticed how often retired heads of corps of engineers have humorous daughters?)

And this former commanding officer of an elite corps had nothing to live on but the meager pension that the rapacious state allocates to its old servants.

The little girl, while still young, had boldly grasped the bull of existence by the horns:

"Because," the cutie said to herself, "because I have no dowry, and refuse to sink to the level of a prostitute, like so many others, I will attempt to embrace a career that is both independent and remunerative."

The intrepid maiden had passed her two baccalaureates,

and now here she was, studying medicine.

The austerity of her studies lent to her pretty face somewhat the appearance of a serious young man. Her eyes, at times, showed the pale gleam of the revenue of it all, which suited her to perfection.

Charming scholaress, how I would have loved you!

Unfortunately, it was he, the somewhat stupid young man, who met her on the stairs and fell in love with her.

Love at first sight? No. However, one day when Alfred (let's call him Alfred to avoid the periphrasis that is always so difficult to vary in a story of this length), one day, as I was saying, when Alfred had little appetite, his mama (a round and fat mama) had said to him:

"You're not eating, Alfred? Are you in love, by any chance?"

Alfred had blushed, as red as a rooster.

So it was settled. Poor Alfred was hooked, and all too aware of his flame!

From then on, he watched for the arrivals and departures of the demoiselle. He followed her, oh, discreetly! on the opposite sidewalk, and that was how he discovered that the young lady reported daily to the School of Medicine to drink the words of the masters.

This observation never ceased to stir a vague terror in the poor lad's soul.

A student! A scholar! What would he ever find to say

to her?

But one Sunday, when he saw her descending the stairs with her old commander of a father, he thought he could tell, from a glance, that she was kind, and hope reflowered in the bower of his heart.

Alfred was correct: Valentine (her name was Valentine), Valentine enjoyed a heart of gold.

A heart of gold, and a shrewdness of amber.

At once, she had guessed the passion of which she was the object.

The information that she gathered, without appearing to, was favorable. And besides (for let us not demean, in our bias, her pure motives), the somewhat foolish air of the handsome lad did not displease her, quite the contrary.

It was at the corner of the boulevard Saint-Michel and the boulevard Saint-Germain that the explanation occurred, during a traffic jam.

At the moment when Alfred least expected it, Valentine took two steps toward him, planted in his two eyes her frank and gentle gaze, held out her hand, and said:

"So do you love me a little, monsieur?"

"But, mademoiselle!…" blushed Alfred.

And Valentine continued, parodying, without remorse, a well-known song:

"If you have something to say to me, why do you go away from me?"

The very next day after that traffic jam, Alfred was admitted to begin his courtship of Valentine.

At the beginning, it did not go smoothly: Alfred, intimidated by his fiancée's intellectual superiority, had nothing to say.

And then, from time to time, unwittingly, the young lady perplexed her betrothed with disconcertingly technical details.

Thus, one morning, when, probably impatient for the great day, his eyes were shining, Valentine asked him point-blank:

"Do you know why, at certain moments, our eyes shine with unaccustomed brightness?"

"???" stammered Alfred.

"Well! I'll tell you. As Von Barensprung so justly remarked, in his *Untersuchungen zur Naturlehre des Menschen und der Tiere,* when the eye shines with happiness or passion, it's because it's filled and stretched by the humors. The globe of the eye, bulging more than usual, projects further from the orbital cavity and reflects more light."

"Ah!"

Poor Alfred!

A few days after this little lesson in physiology, one of his friends complimented him on his fiancée.

"I hope," he added, "that you're not too shy to offer her a little madrigal from time to time?"

"A madrigal!"

This was an utter revelation to the honest Alfred. A madrigal!

"Why, yes!" continued the obliging friend. "You could, for example, compliment her on her large eyes, her small mouth, etc."

Alfred's imagination worked hard on this information.

One fine evening, in the salon, when the young couple found themselves alone, Alfred took his fiancée's hand in his, and said to her:

"My dear Valentine, your eyes are so large and your mouth so small, that if you decided to swallow one of your eyes, you'd have to cut it into at least four pieces."

Valentine kissed Alfred for his trouble.

. . . .

Now, they're married, and without a doubt will soon acquire a batch of children who will all have eyes as big as that, and very small mouths.

A FUNNY IDEA

Yesterday morning, in my voluminous daily mail, I found a note conceived thusly:

"Dear sir and old pal,

In spite of your most sacred principles, come dine with me and a few jolly fellows, this evening. We meet at seven o'clock, on the terrace of the African.

Bring, if you like, a special someone, provided that she be as lovely as the day, or simply fun-loving and devoid of all prejudice, social, worldly, or otherwise. It's up to you!

Your old,

TIROUARD-DELATABLE (de Nuits)."

"What's he up to?" I thought.

For a year ago Tirouard had married a charming woman whom he adored, and without whom he would never go out and have a good time. And I thought again:

"What's he up to?"

I was careful, however, not to miss the meeting. As for bringing a "special someone," it would be a poor assessment of the writer of these lines to think him capable of such conduct. The special someones of others are quite sufficient.

I shall not describe our bacchanal. Let it suffice you to know that the life of Riley himself, beside the one that we led, would have seemed a veritable monastic existence.

At the height of the debauch, one of us asked:

"But finally, O Tirouard-Delatable (de Nuits), what made you decide to offer us this gala?"

"Ah yes, it's true. I forgot to tell you… My wife is very ill at the moment; it appears that she will not even survive the night… So I had the idea of joyfully burying my life as a husband."

The party took off again in full force, and when we separated, the blue morning was effacing the stars.

A GOOD SENTRY REWARDED

Christmas! Christmas! Good Lord, but it was cold!

The men on guard crowd around a stove that snores like a deaf man.

The men are all content, because the night to come is Christmas Eve, and they will eat grilled sausages and drink white wine.

The joyous second-class soldier, Viscount Guy de La Hurlotte, has announced:

"Because I'm on guard tonight, this Christmas Eve, this is my treat."

Eyes shining, the whole guard replied: "Hurray for La Hurlotte!"

That's all well and good, but doesn't change the fact that it's damnably cold.

"Now the snow is falling!" announces Labroche, coming in from the cold.

Yes, the snow is falling. It's falling as if it were raining the stuff. It's falling, it's falling, it's falling. And the men crowd even more around the stove, which they fill with oil.

❀

Ten o'clock.

It's time to go relieve the sentries.

The corporal of the guard, lazy and delicate, wonders why he should go freeze himself. Bah! The new recruits can go relieve their comrades by themselves. Christmas Eve is no time to make the rounds!

The poor soldier Baju sadly heads for the powder magazine, where his sentry duty calls him.

Brrr! It won't be pleasant at the powder magazine, from ten o'clock to midnight.

Let's hope that the others, at headquarters, don't eat all the sausages and drink all the white wine, during that time!

Sad and freezing sentry duty.

The snow begins falling in flurries.

Baju wraps himself up, and takes shelter as well as he can.

One after another, every clock in the village tolls, with agonizing slowness, the quarter hours, the half hours, the hours.

The churches ring for midnight mass.

And since the snow muffles all sounds on the ground, one can even hear, from far away, the church bells out in the country.

Poor Baju's eyes fill with tears: one of those faraway bells sounds exactly like the bell of his church, his own, out there, in the country.

And it is, for Baju, a clear and sudden evocation of his

mother and his two little sisters, kneeling in the village church, praying the good Lord that the poor boy not be too unhappy, and, above all, that he return soon.

Midnight!

And even past midnight!

Baju starts to think that the others don't relieve him very often.

Will there be any sausages left? Will there be any white wine left? Cruel enigma!

Everywhere around him, Baju sees spread out, on the deserted area around the powder magazine, a big white coat of deep snow.

Not to mention that it's still falling.

"Ah!… There's someone!… Damn!… It's not a soldier… It's an old man."

A poor old man who must be frightened, out in weather like this.

His big gray coat doesn't look too luxurious, and his handsome silver hair is no substitute for a good hood.

Already moved by his vision of the country, the church, his mother, and his little sisters, Baju feels his heart flooded with tenderness and pity.

"Come in, old fellow, you'll feel better than out in the snow."

And, removing his sentry coat, he drapes it over the old

man, who thanks him in a deep soft voice.

As for Baju, he stamps his feet in the cold snow, happy to do a favor for the poor old man.

A lull in the storm.

"Many thanks, my friend," says the old man as he leaves, "your good deed will bring you luck."

And the quarter and half hours continue to fall, as if in despir, from the village belfries!

Finally! What a disgrace!

Isn't it shameful to relieve a man at five to one, instead of midnight!

Labroche, who relieves Baju, is abominably drunk, a circumstance which revives Baju's worries about the sausages and the white wine.

They must have had quite a party!

They did indeed! Oh, the pigs!

Everyone at headquarters, from the drummer to the sergeant, as drunk as a Polish headquarters, sprawls pell-mell on the cots.

The sausages no longer exist except in the form of a rather strong aroma.

The wine bottles are so dry, you'd think they were baked in the oven.

Oh yes, the pigs! They can't be such pigs!

And they're all snoring like Dutch tops, on the day after

the kermesse.

Baju stokes the dying fire, and takes off his boots to warm his poor frozen feet.

It feels good, a good fire!

The heat makes Baju drowsy, and Baju dozes off.

And when Baju awakes, and wants to put on his boots again, he sees that someone put something in them. What?

Baju seizes the right boot, and observes the presence of round and metallic objects, which shine.

One louis, two louis, three louis, four louis, five louis!

Five brand-new gold louis!

Baju, far too honest to place this sum in his wallet, stores it in his cartridge belt, for the time being.

The left boot contains three packages wrapped in paper: one big and two small.

The big one is a knife with thirty-two blades, infinitely more superb than the ones he admires every day in the cutler's window on Grand'Rue.

The little packages, they're two pairs of earrings, as cute as anything, for his little sisters, by God!

And then finally, Baju finds a visiting card bearing these words:

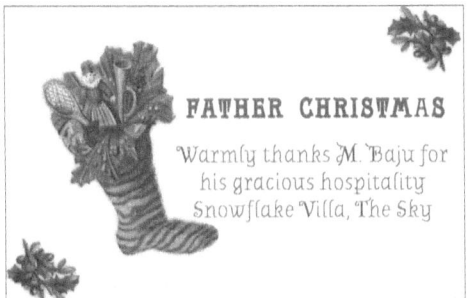

FATHER CHRISTMAS

Warmly thanks M. Baju for
his gracious hospitality
Snowflake Villa, The Sky

BIZARROID

I am not what one would call an enemy of originality. Certainly, I think it's better to wear your own shoes, rather than someone else's. But from there, good God! To slip on the slingbacks of Chimera, the clodhoppers of the Never Lived, or the work boots of the Unhappenable, do you not see a slight nuance?

Certain people strive for every disconcertance. For others too—let us be fair—the bughouse column appears to be the only norm, in Word as well as Deed.

This morning I went to take a bath. At the entrance, two men were chatting, one leaving, and one entering, and the conversation ended on this phrase spoken by the one who was arriving:

"Well, I can assure you, my dear usurer, that I don't have the funds they say I do, because *there's a friend of my Aunt Morin who acts as my former prefect.*"

I could not even dream of guessing the meaning of this remark, but—I will admit—it caused me some uneasiness.

In fact, the man who had proffered this curious phrase occupied the cabin (is it called a cabin when it's for a hot bath?) next to mine.

The walls of my bathhouse are as thin as a balloon.

Therefore, the slightest splash could be heard.

My neighbor, the nephew of Madame Morin, led a hellish existence in his bathtub. One would have thought there was an important meeting of sea lions.

And then, at one moment, he interrupts to ring for the attendant.

"Monsieur rang?" this last soon asks.

"Yes… *Please bring me change for twenty sous.*"

Even now, I still ask myself what pressing need would impel a naked man sitting in lukewarm water to demand, without delay, change for twenty sous.

POOR CESARINE!

If you would like some information on this Alcide Paquet who will be in question, I offer it perfectly willingly.

Alcide Paquet was a big guy around thirty-six or thirty-seven, who lived in Pont-Audemer, on the road to Périgueux, three houses past the customs house.

Physically and morally, Alcide offered nothing to distinguish him from other mortals, except perhaps an extraordinarily common appearance and an extraordinarily uncommon mediocrity.

To support himself, he was the representative for a large company of chemical fertilizers.

On its vast warehouses, huge letters spelled out: *Storehouse for Super-Phosphates, Sal Ammoniac Supply, Special Nitrates, Peruvian Guano*, etc., etc.

Alcide sold a great deal of this productive filth to agriculturalists, but without understanding the poetry of his profession. Never did he ask himself, anxiously, by what mysterious elaboration these ridiculous products become the fine wheat that nourishes good people, the sweet alfafa so dear to livestock, the canola from which we press oil, and the thousands of little yellow, blue, pink, and mauve flowers that enamel our prairies, and which are so pretty that one weeps just to look at them.

If you want my opinion: Alcide Paquet was a stupid lout.

He lived in the house mentioned above, alone with a cousin who also served as his housekeeper, and who was called Mademoiselle Césarine.

Césarine, having lost her parents when she was little, had been taken in by Madame Paquet (Alcide's mother), who, in the charitable intention of transforming her, eventually, into an excellent cleaning lady, had made her, for the moment, into a little all-purpose maid.

Poor Césarine!

Sweet and affectionate by nature, Césarine accepted her role, a smile on her lips.

"Césarine," said Madame Paquet, "when one is penniless, one must get used to work… Shine the shoes."

And Césarine shined the shoes.

"Césarine," repeated Madame Paquet, "when one is penniless, one must get used to work… Wash the dishes."

And Césarine washed the dishes, always with a smile on her lips.

Césarine grew up amid these domestic occupations, and became an accomplished young woman.

The years continued to flow, and Césarine, gradually, changed into an old maid of about thirty.

But still so charming and so fresh!

Her skin especially, one of those pretty skins that are so

delicate you dare not kiss it, but which you kiss anyway!

Poor Césarine!

At this juncture—or at another juncture, I can't be sure—Mother Paquet died, and Father Paquet too.

Alcide said to his cousin:

"Would you like to stay with me?... You can be my housekeeper."

Césarine answered yes, with such eagerness! For—I suppose I can tell you, now that she's dead—she loved her cousin.

And she even loved him secretly, but ferociously; beneath her neatly parted hair, Césarine hid a nature to burst all of Le Creusot's pyrometers.

And Alcide—oh, the lout!—who didn't notice a thing!

As long as he sold plenty of "chemicals" to the farmers, he was content, and there ended his ideal. Poor Césarine!

One evening, Alcide came home all cheerful.

"My little Césarine," he said, as he unfolded his napkin, "this is it!"

"What?... What is it?"

"I'm getting married."

Césarine simply said "Ah!", but the blush in her cheeks suddenly faded.

A great blow had struck her heart, and her eyelids fluttered.

She thought that she would faint.

However, she had the strength to ask:

"And… to whom?"

"Guess."

"To Aline Leproult, perhaps?"

"No."

"To Jeanne Beaudon, perhaps?"

"Exactly!"

That evening, Césarine ate no dinner, and Alcide—what a lout, decidedly!—never noticed a thing.

Poor Césarine!

The evening before the wedding, on the last day that Alcide dined as a bachelor, Césarine's cooking smelled particularly good.

"Oh!" remarked Alcide. "You'll make me regret my decision!"

What smelled so good was a little dish, prepared in a pan, on a wood fire (Césarine always had contempt for gas and for all your modern stoves).

There were fried onions, thyme, and everything!

Parsley, freshly picked and cut up fine, made the dish like the countryside, succulent, aromatic, and smoking.

There was meat that was both firm and tender.

Not beef, not veal, not mutton… What, then?

It wasn't pork, either.

"What is this?" asked Alcide. "What can be as good as this?"

"Is it good?" Césarine simply replied.

"Never, do you hear me, my little Césarine, NEVER have I eaten anything so exquisite."

"Then, that's the important thing."

"You don't want to tell me what it is?"

"Do you insist?"

"Yes."

"Well then!"

Césarine brusquely unhooked her blouse, pushed her undershirt aside, and under her left breast—a marvel of a left breast!—Alcide could see a wound gaping there, critical, bleeding.

At the same time, Césarine fell stone dead onto the floor.

She rose only to say, in English, in a broken voice:

"It is my heart that you have just eaten!"

Poor Césarine!

ET VERBUM...

For some time, young Lily (five years old) had been badgering her poor mother for permission to attend mass with the maid.

Saturday, her mother—a charming woman subject to headaches, note that detail—had told Lily:

"Oh! You're so annoying with your mass, my poor child! Go tomorrow and stop bothering me!"

Lily is radiant. She doesn't sleep that night. At the crack, the very crack, of dawn, she awakens the maid.

And off they go to a morning mass.

Lily takes the keenest pleasure in this novelty. The priest and the choirboy charm her with their costumes of gold, lace, and purple. The hieratic maneuvers of these characters intrigue her to the utmost. The consumption of the sacrifice scandalizes her a little: she finds the priest who drinks his white wine with his back to everyone lacking in manners.

But, above all, the communion of the faithful amuses her the most.

And, at breakfast, when questioned on the subject, Lily explains:

"Well then, it's like this: there were all these nice ladies who walked up to the front and then went down on their knees. Then the priest came around with a big gold bowl, and then he put an aspirin tablet in the mouths of all the nice ladies."

THE HENRI II CHEST

We had come to that moment in the dinner that usually produces an explosion of generous sentiments.

With one accord, we lambasted slavery. The question had been put on the table by a tubby fellow who was thought to be the natural son of Monsignor Lavigerie. (The fact is that the extreme rubicundness of his complexion seemed to derive directly from some cardinalesque crimson.)

The dinner was a joyous dinner, consisting of a few Portuguese, who, as an Arabian proverb affirms, never engender melancholy.

There was Major Saligo, and Timeo Danaos, and Dona Ferentès (the only woman in the company), and Sinon, and Vero, and Ben Trovato, and a few others that I'm forgetting.

By way of Frenchmen: the scarlet bastard, the Navy lieutenant Becque-Danlot, and myself.

I said above that we lambasted slavery with one accord; that is not exactly accurate. Becque-Danlot lambasted nothing whatsoever. Becque-Danlot seemed, for the moment, a stranger to all indignation.

It was the beautiful Dona Ferentès who noticed it first.

"Well, Captain!" she said in her pretty Andalusian voice. "Doesn't it revolt you, those men sold by other men, those hideous markets in Africa?"

"I ask a thousand pardons, señora," replied the man of the sea. "I am indignant to the core of my being, but my past conduct prohibits me from joining you in publicly decrying these detestable practices."

After a pause, he added:

"I, who speak to you now, I have sold a man!"

The memory did not seem to torment excessively our friend Becque-Danlot, for he let out a laugh in which remorse subtracted nothing from its joyous sonority.

"You, Captain! You, the honor of the French Navy! You have sold a man?"

"I have sold a man!" insisted Becque-Danlot, still laughing.

"In Africa?"

"No, not in Africa, in France."

"In France!"

"Precisely! And even better: in Paris."

"In Paris!"

"Precisely! And even better: in the auction house on rue Drouot."

At that, we decided that the intrepid sailor was mocking us.

The natural son of Monsignor Lavigerie spoke for all of us:

"You're pulling our leg, Captain!"

Without acknowledging this vulgar apostrophe,

Becque-Danlot continued:

"Yes, señora, yes, gentlemen, I have disposed of a man at the auction house. It wasn't even a brilliant transaction I made there. I even lost 350 francs… but I had a good laugh."

A question mark drew itself on each of our faces.

"Tell me about it," ordered Ferentès.

A French soldier has never refused anything to a grand Andalusian lady: the fact is well known.

I silently omit the classic cigar lit by the storyteller, the traditional bluish spirals that he contemplated for a moment, and I proceed to Becque-Danlot's story:

This was all three years ago. I arrived from Senegal with six months of convalescent leave, fully intending to profit greatly from it.

A small inheritance I had just received allowed me to do things properly. I rented, on rue Brémontier, a ground floor that I furnished quite nicely, my word, and there I was ready for the joyful life.

One evening, at the Jardin-de-Paris, I made the acquaintance of a young woman who suited me enormously. Not amazingly pretty, but with such distinction and charm! Very reserved, in addition, and bearing no resemblance to all the merchants of love who populated the place.

She told me some nonsensical story, which I cut off, besides, as with a razor.

Daughter of a general, raised in Saint-Denis, father

remarried, shrewish stepmother, constant quarrels, impossible existence, flight, unhappiness, suicidal thoughts.

All accompanied by furtive tears that she blotted frequently with a handkerchief that smelled very good.

What happened next, you've all guessed, haven't you? I brought the young person home with me, I installed her, provided her with a little darling of a maid.

In short, I was good to her, as if it were going out of style, and discreet, and polite. Completely charming, I tell you.

I left her alone almost all day, only coming to pick her up in the evening, around six o'clock, for dinner, to go to the theater, to a concert.

She seemed to have conceived an ardent passion for me, and often repeated to me:

"When you leave me, my friend, I will kill myself."

Damn!

I was starting to become seriously concerned over the direction things were taking, when, one morning, the little darling of a maid gave me a note that she asked I read later, during the day:

"Monsieur," said the note, "has no idea how little Madame cares for Monsieur. Monsieur has no sooner turned on his heels, than Madame welcomes a sort of gigolo, who looks terribly shady.

"Should Monsieur return suddenly, which has already

happened once, the plan is in place: the gigolo slips into the Henri II chest that serves as a wood box in the winter. Madame locks the chest, drops the key in her pocket, and nobody is the wiser. Since the lid doesn't fit very well, and the chest is very large, the gigolo is not too uncomfortable, while Monsieur is there.

"To be sure to catch the gigolo, it's best to come at around two o'clock in the afternoon.

MARIE."

At first, I refused to believe in such villainy, but all the same I was there at around two o'clock.

An expressive gesture from the little darling of a maid told me I had arrived at the right time.

Ellen (did I tell you that the woman's name was Ellen?), Ellen welcomed me with her most enchanting smile, and her calmest expression.

"What a pleasure to see you at this hour!"

The key of the chest was not in the lock, a big wrought iron key of the period, rather difficult to conceal.

A few liberties with my hands told me beyond a doubt that the key was in one of the beauty's pockets.

So no more doubt!

How the idea came to me to do what I did, in that circumstance, I still don't know. A flash of genius, no doubt!

I sent Ellen to buy me a tie from a shirtmaker on the

avenue de Villier, claiming she alone could choose one to my taste.

During her absence, and in less time than it takes to write it, I hailed a car, and, with the help of a delivery boy, loaded the Henri II chest into it, and then off to the auction house.

The trunk, thanks to a few judiciously distributed hundred sou coins, took its place in a set of furniture about to be put on sale.

There were a few objections about the missing key, but the condition of the outside attested to the preservation of the interior.

After a half hour, a man from Auvergne made its acquisition for the sum of 250 francs. (It had cost me 600.)

My chest was loaded, with its contents, onto an enormous moving van. The most miscellaneous objects were piled on top of it, bedding, bronze statues, bottles of wine, birdcages, baby carriages, glass chandeliers, etc.

Under all this paraphernalia, the gigolo must have been having a hellish time, but the thick sides of the chest muffled his cries.

In what direction was he taken? Was he quickly set at liberty? Or is he still in there? I never dreamed of bothering myself with those details; but I repeat, señora and gentlemen, if I have ever laughed in my life, it was on that day.

As for Ellen, I never saw her again.

The little darling of a maid told me that she had left my

apartment after collecting a little package of her valuables, and without making the slightest allusion to the missing trunk.

Since that time, I have banned all Henri II chests from my furnishings.

THE FAMILY TRICK

I have never dreamed of claiming that the single life does not offer a thousand distinctive advantages, whose enumeration would lead me far afield.

But beside these profits, how many little ineluctable miseries, how many moral inferiorities, how many discouraging disappointments!

Say what you will, there are a hundred feats forbidden to a bachelor, which are mere child's play for a family.

The other day I witnessed a whole little comedy that literally delighted me, and which—I must admit—strongly incited me to wed and to procreate.

Having arrived a little late, I found the train almost full. As my trip was rather long, my face grew even longer, at the thought that there were no more good corners to spare.

My attention was immediately drawn to two small children, a boy and a girl, making an infernal racket with their trumpets in the doorway to a compartment.

Behind them, standing, a woman with her shirt unbuttoned more than necessary was nursing a newborn, who howled like a young demon.

A gentleman—the father, obviously, and the husband— stayed in the back, smoking his pipe enough to make the locomotive jealous.

I quickly made up my mind, so charmed was I with this pretty family scene. I entered.

To say that I was welcomed with a unanimous smile would be an obvious exaggeration. On the contrary, my arrival provoked on every face a hideous rictus of discontent.

A blow of the whistle, and off we went.

Then, a transformation scene.

The father returns his pipe to its case.

The mother reswaddles the baby, places it carefully in the luggage rack, and returns a bit of order to the economy of her blouse.

The two older children abandon their trumpets, and settle into a corner, as good as gold.

The whole group falls asleep, except me, amazed at this sudden tranquility.

The tranquility lasted until we approached the next station.

At that moment, a new transformation scene, and a renewal of hostilities.

The pipe, the mama unbuttoned, the little one screaming, the kids blowing their trumpets.

And then the train took off again. Peace, silence, sleep.

So it was at every station until Brussels, where I got off, in the chance company of those people.

I beg you to believe that not a single traveler thought of

invading our compartment.

And I suspected—perhaps correctly—that the gentleman with the pipe had married and had created children for the sole purpose of driving away from his compartment, when he was traveling, all intruders.

A NEW POET

When cake is served, Trice likes a slice.
Today I had to ask him twice.
Why, Trice?

When I invited Twine to dine,
He answered with a vulgar sign.
Why, Twine?

My teacher, Tout, just gave a shout
And then began to run about.
Why, Tout?

This little poem, which I have just quoted in its entirety, is entitled "Solicitudes," and has as its author M. Franc-Nohain.

As you might imagine, Franc-Nohain is only a pseudonym (which conceals one of the most excellent prefects of our Third Republic).

Of the personality of the poet, I will say nothing, in the quite legitimate fear of injuring my chances for promotion. But I own a copy of the Work, and would have to consider myself quite a naughty little boy indeed if I did not bring it to the attention of my charming readers and my very nice readeresses.

The literary baggage of Franc-Nohain consists of a certain number of little poems, all of a rare intensity and none too voluminous, as you have been able to judge by "Solicitudes."

For, in fact, nothing would have prevented our bard from also asking why Trussian, why Twotter, why Telephant.

He uses discretion. Let us praise him for it.

The ideas that make up the basis of Franc-Nohain's poems are, in general, bizarre, unexpected, and so very evocative! The artist has been able to free himself from repellent and outdated formulas. When, by chance, he meets an alexandrine, you can rest assured that he could not do otherwise, and is upset by it.

One of the first things I read by this poet was his "Dance of the Careless Nephews." It gave me such pleasure, at the time, that I beg your permission to quote it in full. It concerns several young men whose uncles have disappeared, following, no doubt, some vile debauch. The nephews speak:

> We have checked in all the provincial bars,
> We have scoured the plains and every hill;
> We have seen the boats stand still,
> And we have seen the stopping of the cars;
> But the boats have sailed on
> And the cars are also gone;
> Under the quincunxes,
> We cannot find our uncles.

On Friday we did not get our wish,
We went there every Sunday,
Tuesday, Wednesday, Thursday, Monday,
And it was not a different kettle of fish;
It is probable that if we had gone every Saturday
We would have the same thing to say;
Under the quincunxes,
We cannot find our uncles.

Certainly, these verses are not quite Corneille, but what an admirable evocation of modern life! Nothing is omitted! In other words, there it is!

That, from time to time, a few improbabilities crop up in Franc-Nohain's work, I cannot deny. The following tale, among others, is perfectly unacceptable (I cite only those excerpts indispensable to the understanding of the story);

I knew, in my youth, an elderly lapidary
Who had purchased a very large dromedary,
Unfortunately, the lapidary had to put it in the commode,
Because he had such a small abode.
And then, the poor dromedary,
Suffocated, because it wasn't very airy.

A bit, in the same vein, from "The Song of the Porcupine":

It was a little porcupine
That I found, one evening, on my doormat, rue Constantine.

M. Franc Nohain recounts, then, that he studies the young animal, asks if it really wants to enter his house, if there is not some mistake. When it makes no answer, the poet continues:

> It was then that I noticed that it had passed away.
> And at that point, you understand, I had nothing more to say.

Bourgeois life is equally interesting to Franc-Nohain. One encounters a few scenes, neatly turned, in his work. The "Complaint of Monsieur Benoît" is to be cited. Unfortunately, I lack the space.

It concerns a Monsieur Benoît who commits suicide

> In his pretty house in the Saint-Mandé countryside.

Poor Madame Benoît! Poor Junior Benoît! etc., etc.

> Poor little Mademoiselle Benoît is to be pitied, in all candor,
> For she was set to marry a rich businessman in Indre.

And the poet closes in this way:

> Nevertheless, the whole family accompanied him to the cemetery,
> For on such an occasion their presence is customary.

Franc-Nohain's latest production charmed me more than

I can say. It is dedicated to "Our Maeterlinck," and entitled "The Toothpicks Remember and Sing."

In this exquisitely intimate little poem, the artist employs the following fiction: the toothpicks that have come from goose feathers, as everyone knows, encounter in a diner's molars a few fragments of the fowl from which they were extracted.

> And then we recall
> That evening last fall
> Back when some friendly servant had the chore
> Of plucking our poor mother by the door.
> And when I close my eyes, I see
> The simple joys of country life,
> The hedge in bloom, the apple tree,
> The farmer and his loving wife.
> (As Hégésippe Moreau so ingeniously put it.)
> In restaurants where the menu is prix fixe,
> We are the sad and melancholy toothpicks.

Does not all that have a very persuasive charm?

M. Franc-Nohain has suffered greatly in life, one can tell. May heaven grant that he suffer much more, so that we can enjoy the pleasure of reading him longer.

A PETITION

Quite recently, M. Onézime Lahilat, a peaceful little rentier in Pourd-sur-Alaure (Haute-Toucque), returned from the station, where he had gone to watch the train from Paris pass and to acquire his newspaper.

Having arrived at the tinsmith's that adjoins the Café de la Poste, M. Onézime Lahilat suffered a relatively serious accident.

A terrine shattered on the external part of his right calf, and all the contents of the same (dirty water and organic detritus) spread upon the light chamois trousers of the poor gentleman.

A woman of a certain age, the legitimate spouse of the tinsmith who had caused the catastrophe, found nothing better to do, at this irritating event, than to hold her sides with all her available hands.

Similarly, an apprentice laughed noisily, showing his wolfish teeth.

Less indignant at the misfortune itself than at the inappropriate gaiety it had provoked among these people of low intellectual attainment, M. Onézime Lahilat, with a checkered handkerchief, stanched the disaster, murmuring:

"It seems to me you could be more careful."

Emerged then the tinsmith in person, claiming in acrimonious mode:

"Well, you senile old fool, when someone empties a terrine on the sidewalk, just go across the street."

"I shall do that from now on," M. Onézime Lahilat contented himself with replying, offended but dignified.

And that was what he did from then on, as he had said.

He, whose habit it was to walk to the station on the left sidewalk of the Grand'Rue, and to return on the left sidewalk, adopted the uncivilized custom of confining himself to the right sidewalk, wheresoever he might come, and wheresoever he might go.

And then, a dilemma budded near his heart.

Did he really have the right to confine himself, after a trivial quarrel, to one side of the street, rather than to the other?

Wasn't he being a little irresponsible?

Like a buoy, what am I saying? like a shipwreck, foundercd his moral sense, as a citizen, a voter, a taxpayer.

Soon, he could stand it no longer, and, one fine day, upon a pure and spacious sheet of ministerial paper, he addressed a petition to M. Carnot, President of the French Republic.

Explicated at length, respectfully formulated, the factum concluded with this:

"...In consequence of the facts expressed above, the undersigned humbly requests from the head of state the authorization to walk exclusively on the sidewalk to the right of the Grand'Rue of Pourd-sur-Alaure (Haute-Toucque)."

Fortunately, France possesses at its head M. Carnot, a serious fellow who attends to business, and who insists that everything pass through his own hands, as he says in his picturesque language.

And is that not better, between us, for the health of the supreme executive as well as for the interest of the country, than to have to contend with a President of the Republic who goes out carousing, until two or three in the morning, in the cafés of Montmartre!

Upon reading M. Onézime Lahilat's petition, M. Carnot could not suppress his keen interest.

"What do you think, Kornprobst?"

"But," politely replied the man of the sea, "I am precisely, on this question, of the same opinion as you, my president."

"My opinion, is that this is more Loubet's business than mine."

M. Kornprobst struck a gong, and a republican guard on horseback appeared.

"Take this to the Interior," ordered M. Kornprobst, with that arrogance affected by naval officers whenever they have anything to do with the land forces.

And he added:

"Tell Loubet to get busy… It's urgent."

The republican guard on horseback would not trouble his mount for such a little errand. (If it's fifty meters from the Elysée to the place Beauveau, it's a mile.)

M. Loubet acquainted himself with M. Onézime Lahilat's petition.

"M. Carnot means well," he murmured, "but sometimes he assigns me tasks that should not be mine. This story is more the concern of the prefect of Haute-Tocque."

And requesting pen and paper, M. Loubet forwarded to the aforementioned official papa Onézime's petition, urging him to get on top of the situation.

The prefect of Haute-Toucque was doing just that with a cocotte from Paris, when he received the message from his hierarchical superior.

"But," he interrupted, "what the hell does this have to do with me, this business! It concerns the mayor of Pourd-sur-Alaure. Send me a gendarme!"

"Present!" said a martial voice.

It was the gendarme.

"And above all, gendarme, tell the mayor not to let the grass grow on this stratagem, eh?"

(He used the word "stratagem" just to impress the gendarme.)

On receipt of the missive, the mayor's face became as a pale as a serpent's.

"I hope," he thought, "that this affair won't prevent me from being decorated on January 1!"

It was late.

The cream of Pourd-sur-Alaure society was going to dinner.

To make a decision himself never even crossed the mayor's mind.

He summoned to his office a police officer (an "usher," as they call them), and gave him fifteen or so little bulletins, summoning the city's municipal councillors to a special meeting.

Nobody was missing, except for one who was deceased. The mayor brought the gentlemen up to date on the question, and a lively discussion ensued.

It was close to midnight when the meeting was adjourned.

We are fortunate in being able to give our readers the final "considerings" of the Council's decision:

"Considering, etc., etc.;

"Considering that the grounds invoked by the aforementioned Onézime Lahilat do not appear to be sufficiently warranted, and that such an example would set a dangerous precedent;

"Considering that the legislature placed two sidewalks on the roads so that they may be used equally;

"Considering that if the population of Pourd-sur-Alaure developed the habit of walking on one sidewalk to the detriment of the other, and reciprocally, etc., etc.;

"The Municipal Council of Pourd-sur-Alaure does not authorize the aforementioned Onézime Lahilat to walk exclusively on the sidewalk to the right of the Grand'Rue."

AN AUTUMNAL CLICHE

A typesetter at my paper has just announced to me that the cliché "We return… We have returned," is not as hackneyed as one might think, and that it can still serve another time or two.

God knows, however, whether we have overused this Paris that returns, that never stops returning!

It begins in the first days of September, and never ends.

When I was just a little boy (oh, what I pretty little boy I made, sweet, friendly, and how nasty deep inside!) and I read the gossip columns in the big magazines, I imagined "Paris that returns" in such a funny way!

Trunks that could house whole families, hatboxes more innumerable than the pebbles on the shore, stationmasters losing their heads, and above all—oh! above all!—beautiful young women a bit tired from the trip, but so charming, once rested, tomorrow.

Nothing true, in all of that.

The train that arrives today at 6:20 bears an astonishing resemblance to the train that arrived, three months ago, at 7:15, and one could easily mistake it for the train that will arrive in six months at a quarter to noon.

As for the people who were in Trouville this summer, or

on their own land, this fall, they were replaced in Paris by other people who were in Nice this winter, or in whatever next spring.

Especially in Paris, nobody is indispensable.

Paris returns!… Paris goes away!…

And then what? If I were the rude type, I know what I'd say.

I too, I returned a few days ago, and found, on my desk, a stack of letters, without exaggeration, as high as that.

If I had to answer them personally, I would have to mobilize the entire reserve and land forces of all the secretaries in France.

So, what did I do? I will answer, I decided, just one, taken at random.

The lucky winner proved to be a young painter, who asked me what he should do, when he wanted to work, to drive from his studio all the pests, bores, borrowers, salesmen, and other amateurs.

Oh, my God! It's quite simple! Let this artist follow my example, and he will be content.

Three years ago, I had installed, at the entrance to my vestibule, a turnstile through which one had to pass to reach me.

A disabled soldier in my employ demands the preliminary payment of the sum of one franc.

You have no idea, ever since that initiative, how my horde

of visitors has diminished!

The bores think it over. Paying twenty sous to annoy people is often not their prerogative.

The borrowers are, for the most part, eliminated. The only ones that enter are the high-flying borrowers (in the 25,000 range). Those, I let them talk.

As for the creditors, they never hesitate. What is twenty sous to a creditor?

Me, I don't stop them.

So, this very morning, I settled a little bill of ninety francs with my bootmaker. He had come twenty-five times. That makes a little over 30 percent.

And besides, I want to organize exclusive days for a hundred sous: Friday, for example.

A NEW ORGAN[1]

If newspapers were founded only when there's a gap to be filled, they would never be founded, or else founded all the time.

The paper I will present to you, ladies and gentlemen, does not seem to be burdened with this claim.

The only pretention that it displays is to be bimonthly: which it justifies amply, for, having appeared about a month ago, it is on its second issue.

It is entitled savagely *The Scalp Hunter*, with this subtitle, not as absurd as it seems: Monitor of the Possible.

Let us hasten to add that in the course of its columns, there is no mention whatsoever of scalps, or hair of any kind, and that the "possible" is not even broached.

To give the reader an idea of this paper, so personal and so amusing, I am forced to publish a few extracts.

If one excepts the question of scalp hunting, no subject is foreign to the editors of *The Scalp Hunter*.

To begin with, a well understood society note that could add something to the paper's coffers:

"The Count and Countess of *** assembled the other day, in their house on rue …, the most elegant and select society.

"The Count of ***, as everyone knows, is a man of the theater in the purest sense of the term, etc.

"Mademoiselle *** was absolutely ideal in the role of ingenue, and M. *** reminded us of Arnal and the great comics of the variety theater. The evening concluded with a cotillion led by M. *** and Mademoiselle ***.

> *(Box seats available.)*"

Another squib destined to be of great interest to high society:

"Our up-to-date dandies no longer send, as they did three years ago, their shirts to London, for, here at home, the art of laundry has made serious progress. But they continue to have their shoes, which they wear unpolished, waxed in Cowes.

"It is only by this means that leather acquires that hard and Britannic shine that has neither the garish insolence of polish nor the notorious gleam of Brazilian footwear."

International reporting holds an important place in *The Scalp Hunter*, which, in this genre, debuted with a masterstroke.

It simply went to interview the Eternal to ask him his frank opinion of the Sâr Péladan.

If that is not international reporting, what is?

A few excerpts from the account of this curious visit:

"The director of this journal, exasperated by the pretensions of M. Joséphin Péladan, wondered if the so-called 'Sâr' really had any valid divine investiture.

"…It was not, in fact, an easy task. It was necessary, first of all, to find God's domicile, and opinions on the matter were sharply divided. It was then necessary to convince the Lord to abandon His constant silence, which, either from natural timidity or a taste for mystery, He seemed sworn to observe.

"…It was thanks to the kindness of an authentic angel, met by chance, and whose name would mean nothing to anyone, that we were able, with the promise of a certain discretion, to learn the Good Lord's address."

The reporter arrives, hands his card to the receiving angel, who introduces him, "politely extinguishing his sword of flame." Portrait of the Good Lord who, respectful of tradition, wears His legendary white beard, and whose pleasant smile, His eyes filled with benevolence, does not contradict His universal reputation for kindness. The eternal indicates to the young man a chair facing his desk:

"…The Creator—He permitted us to call him that— usually stays in the room in which we find ourselves. It's a vast room, lit by two large windows. On each side of the fireplace stand two lamps, which light up, when evening comes, at a simple command from the Lord. On the walls of the office, carefully framed, are displayed drawings of planets, plans for sidereal systems, and also two small unsigned landscapes, with a truly singular audacity of color, and which would certainly cause a sensation in a public exhibit, for they reveal the curious way their author sees and interprets nature."

The reporter respectfully explains the purpose of his visit to the Lord.

After a moment of silence, the latter decides to reply in a voice so sweet that it wrings from the publicist this ineffable reflection: "Ah! What a pity that the Almighty doesn't do His propaganda himself! How quickly popularity would come to Him, just for the charm of that voice!"

"…On the subject of M. Péladan, He told us, My response will be clear. I don't know him any more particularly than any other of his fellow fifteen hundred million earthlings. He therefore has no authority to speak in My name. It is not My habit to issue denials, and it would be a huge task to disavow all those who daily claim to be inspired by Me."

The conversation continues awhile, touching on different subjects. Then, on a somewhat indiscreet request from the reporter, who invites Him, should He have any communications to make, to send them to *The Scalp Hunter*, which would be happy to be His interpreter, the Almighty responds in an evasive manner, and, rising from his seat: "Excuse Me," He says, "several worlds to create…"

I would need to quote all of this drolly imaginative publication.

A theatrical article to end with:

"…We cannot leave the Comédie-Française without announcing the return of *Horace*, with the three Coquelin brothers.

"M. Paul Delair will write, for this occasion, the roles of the second and third Horace, which old Corneille, either by oversight or a lack of enough actors, neglected to put into his work."

If, after these few excerpts, you do not throw yourself upon *The Scalp Hunter*, there is no hope for you. It cannot be found, believe us, at every newsstand; but your bookstore, at your request, will take great pleasure in procuring it for you.

Besides, it would be so simple to subscribe. Here are the prices:

1 year (24 issues): 3 francs.

10 years (240 issues): 28 francs.

100 years (2,400 issues): 200 francs.

No need to underline the advantages of that last offer.

1. Above all, let nobody think that *The Scalp Hunter* emerged piping hot from my imagination.

This organ appeared in the course of 1892. It lasted for three issues.

It has recently reappeared, inserted into the *Revue Blanche*, with, as directors, MM. Tristan Bernard and Pierre Veber.

HAN RYBECK OR, THE STIRRUP CUP AN ICELANDIC STORY

To the only one I love, and who knows it all too well.[1]

I am far from regretting the trip I have just taken to Iceland. I was welcomed by honest people, simple hearts, smelling more of roe than garlic, which does not displease me.

The inhabitants are no stupider than those in southern Europe, and don't shout as loudly.

The food, though none too varied, is healthy and abundant, and one has all the trouble in the world to get the bill. Blessed country!

And besides, the beautiful legends one finds there, and the funny stories, too!

Let me tell you one, slightly altered for Parisian tastes.

It was in the fourteenth century. Iceland groaned under the yoke of the harsh Norwegian duke Polalek VI.

Eager for independence, the young Icelanders had sworn to rid themselves of those brutal and indiscreet foreigners.

Among the rebels, there was one who was known for the stringency of his demands and the uncommon energy of his deeds: he was called Han Rybeck.

Han Rybeck! When Icelanders truly worthy of the name

said "Han Rybeck," they had said it all.

The Norwegian duke Polalek VI had, in a way, deliberately incurred the disfavor of this fine people.

Drunk and ribald, he made a sport of offending the chaste and temperate morals of the Icelandic people, accustomed to love only their wives and to quench their thirst with melting snow.

Obviously, this state of affairs could not long endure.

He imagined, in an hour of intoxication, this ridiculous enterprise, hardly worth a shrug of the shoulders from the most peaceful of men:

On his orders, wolves were brought into the peninsula of Lagrenn-Houyer (which means, in the Finnish language, "land in the shape of a phallus.")

At the entry to the peninsula, supervised men kept guard with pikes and slings, to prevent the wolves from escaping.

Beside the sea, fishermen, in great quantity, were ordered to herd, onto the coast of the pensinsula, as many seals as they could.

In Polalek VI's unbalanced imagination, the meeting of the wolves and the seals would produce a sort of strange hybrid: a wolf that barked like a seal.

Just between us, he was the one who was "barking"!

The poor Icelanders, terrorized, did not dare refuse this

ludicrous command, and all set to work.

At that moment, Han Rybeck was out of the country.

Having left several days ago to go cod fishing (for cod fishing existed back then, and M. Pierre Loti invented nothing), Han Rybeck was not expected back any time soon.

Fortunately, things turned out better than imagined.

One night, the bold fisherman had met an English sloop, loaded with cod, and ready to return to its homeland.

The whole crew was drunk, but drunk as only the English can be drunk when they decide to be drunk.

With a few ably distributed strokes of his axe, Han Rybeck put an end to the whining of those filthy sots. In a twinkling, he transferred the Englishmen's catch into his own boat. The following evening, he arrived, the wind astern, into the port of Reykjavik.

Some of the women filled him in on Polalek's latest scheme, and begged him to intervene.

Ah! It was soon done!

In one leap, he arrived at Lagrenn-Houyer.

In another leap, and armed with a terrible handspike, he dispersed the vile copulations between the seals and the wolves.

In a panic, the animals fled, the seals toward land, the wolves toward the ocean.

Revived by the presence of their leaders, the Icelanders

found new courage. Meanwhile, Polalek VI, warned of these disorders, galloped off on his little pony (Arabian horses are, in that region, difficult to breed).

In less time than it takes to write it (especially when you have a bad pen and almost no ink, like me, at the moment), Han Rybeck was seized, garroted, and thrown into the castle's prison.

Polalek VI, acting as an appeals judge whose decision was final, sentenced him to death, and declared that the execution would take place the next morning, on the very site of the crime.

Han did not protest.

He asked only that he be permitted, before his death, to marry his fiancée, one of the prettiest girls on the island, named Paule Norr.

On the insistence of the bailiff of Reykjavik, a fine man whose name, Fern Anxo, has been preserved by history, Polalek consented to the ceremony.

At daybreak, one hour before the execution, the young lady was led into the condemned man's cell.

The bailiff, representing the registry office², inscribed the names of the young couple.

Completely drunk, Polalek VI performed the religious consecration of their union, and everyone was preparing to leave, including the young bride, when Han Rybeck violently exclaimed:

"Excuse me, excuse me! It was not merely for the sake of formality that I asked to marry my blonde fiancée, Paule Norr."

"What!" said the astonished Polalek. "You want to..."

"Why not?"

(This conversation took place, of course, in Finnish dialect.)

"Well! That's a stiff request," replied the harsh duke.

"You got that right," a courtier wittily observed.

And a coarse laugh shook the brutes.

Not really such a bad man, deep down, Polalek granted the condemned man's final wish.

"Leave them alone!" he ordered.

And, discreetly, everyone withdrew.

After a few moments (the manuscript I have before me does not specify the interval), the door of the cell was opened, and the newlyweds proudly emerged.

Han Rybeck, head held high, one arm tenderly around the waist of the beautiful Paule.

Paule, transfigured, a deep blush suffused across her pretty features, her hair warmer in color, it seemed, and rather tousled. And her large eyes shone as if with recent ecstacy!

This time, Polalek could not conceal his admiration.

"Would you look at that! That's wonderful!" he exclaimed

in the rough language of the North.

Making the sacred sign of benediction over the pair, he pardoned Han Rybeck, gave him the peninsula of Lagrenn-Houyer, and invited the young couple to be fruitful and multiply.

The young couple did not have to be told twice.

1. A useful dedication, which I cannot recommend enough to my colleagues. It costs nothing, and, at the same time, makes five or six people happy.

2. Even in the harshest days of Norwegian domination, the Icelandic towns kept their municipal privileges. The Norwegian *dildøs* only exercised military and ecclesiastical rights.

A NEWS ITEM

Last Thursday, M. and Mme. H… made their way to the Montmartre Theater to attend a performance of *The Old Corporal*. They had left their domicile under the protection of a very intelligent little dog who answered to the name of Castor.

If man is truly the king of creation, the dog can, without fear of exaggeration, be considered the baron, at least.

Castor, in particular, is an extremely remarkable animal, of whom M. and Mme. H… have said many times:

"Castor?… We wouldn't give him up for 10,000 francs!… Even if it were the Pope who asked us for him!"

M. and Mme. H… were very wise in this attachment.

No sooner were those fine people at the second act of *The Old Corporal*, when burglars introduced themselves into their domicile.

Castor, busy at the time playing with a cork in the kitchen, heard the noise, did not recognize those of his masters (the footsteps, of course), and hid in a corner, his ear cocked.

A minute later, his suspicions were confirmed: they were indeed burglars he had to deal with.

To the guile of a fox, Castor added the caution of a serpent combined with the fidelity of a swallow. Only the courage of the lion was missing from this poor animal.

What to do in such an occasion? A fierce anxiety seized Castor's throat.

Bark? What folly! The brigands would throw themselves upon him and strangle him, like a chicken.

Keep quiet? Run away? And what about his professional duty!

A light, probably of genius, suddenly flooded Castor's brain.

As stealthy as a wolf (which was easy for him atavistically, the dog having descended from the wolf), Castor hurried toward a house in construction, lying not far from the H... domicile. Seizing in his teeth one of the lanterns (the Tempest brand, so called because the slightest breeze suffices for its extinction), Castor returned posthaste to the lodgings of his masters.

The ruse had all the success it deserved. The burglars, noticing the light in the next room, thought they had been surprised, and escaped over the rooftops (burglars always escape over the rooftops, whenever surprised).

It would be impossible to describe Castor's joy, on seeing his deception succeed.

When his masters returned, they found him still rubbing his paws in satisfaction.

And there are people who say that animals have no souls! What imbeciles!

EVEN

He—and I do not say "he" lightly—who first stated the lapidary axiom "Good accounts make good neighbors" was by no means a callow youth.

The number of disciples it has guided appears, to me, innumerable. Far from objecting to it, I find myself in complete accord.

One of my friends, whom I had the honor—I believe—of introducing to you here, a few weeks ago, Captain Cap, brings to my thesis the august contingent of his recent example.

Some time last week, as Captain Cap left a meeting of the "General Union of the Whalers of the Corrèze," of which he is vice president, he met a little prostitute, with whom, for the night, he elected to set up housekeeping.

At dawn, he left the young woman, excusing himself—on God knows what pretext—from delivering payment to the courtesan.

Only three or four days later, Captain Cap visited Montmulot Observatory, where he is charged especially with the nocturnal surveillance of conjunctional relations, and again met the young lady from the other day.

Once more he made her acquaintance.

At dawn, as Cap prepared to leave his companion, this

last—and, one might add, at last—had the idea of asking the Captain for money, which, although a nominal sum, still established a troublesome precedent.

So, in his frostiest tones, Cap said:

"Excuse me, mademoiselle: it is true that I slept with you last Monday."

"…"

"Do not interrupt."

"…"

"But did you not also sleep with me, that night?"

"So?"

"So, we are even."

And Cap returned to his little hotel on the rue Jadin, filled with the greatest serenity.

THE MEAT-LAND

At this story, an incredulous smile crossed my lips, and little sparkles of amusement twinkled in my eyes.

My interlocutor showed no reaction, which will not surprise you in the least, when you learn that my interlocutor was none other than Captain Cap, former starter at the Quebec Observatory (it was he who gave the "departure" to shooting stars).

Cap contented himself with summoning the waiter and ordering "two more," which is the American way to say "more of the same," or, more plainly, "another round."

I have known Captain Cap for some time now; I often meet him in one of the many American bars near the Opera House and the Madeleine Church; I am used to his bluff and hyperbole, but this story, really, went beyond the permissible pale of the Canadian joke.

(Canadians are charming children, and, one might say, sort of transatlantic Gascons.)

Cap coldly informed me that they had just discovered, six miles from Arthurville (in the province of Quebec), a cold cut mine!

Yes, I heard that correctly, and you read it correctly: *a cold cut mine*, or "Meat-Land," as they call it there.

I resolved to get to the bottom of this, so the next morning

I paid a call on the Canadian Consulate, at 10, rue de Rome.

In the absence of M. Fabre, the amiable General Agent, I was received—quite graciously, I might add—by his son Paul, and by the honorable Maurice O'Reilly, a young diplomat of great promise.

"Meat-Land!" these gentlemen cried. "Why, nothing could be more serious! What? You don't believe in Meat-Land?"

I had to confess my skepticism.

The two gentlemen were only too happy to catch me up on the matter, and I learned many strange things.

Near Arthurville, in the middle of the virgin forest (it was virgin then), lay an enormous bowl-shaped ravine, ringed by steep cliffs, and carpeted (like our Alps) with a thousand varieties of aromatic plants: thyme, lavender, tarragon, laurel, etc.

The forest was populated by moose, antelopes, deer, rabbits, hares, etc.

On one exceptionally hot and dry day, a fire broke out in the forest, and soon spread throughout the region.

Terrified, the unlucky creatures fled, seeking shelter from the inferno.

There was the ravine, with its steep but incombustible cliffs. The animals thought they were saved!

They had not reckoned on the extraordinary heat unleashed by the tremendous blaze.

Moose, antelopes, deer, rabbits, hares, etc., dove in by the thousands, hoping for refuge, and finding only death by suffocation.

Not only did all this game die, but it was cooked.

Until the temperature dropped back to normal, all of this meat simmered in its own juices (as in the culinary technique we call "braising").

The heavier parts—bones, horns, skin—sank gently to the bottom of the giant pot. The lighter fat floated to the top, forming a sort of protective crust.

Meanwhile, the little aromatic herbs (like those in our Alps) seasoned the pâté, and made it into a succulent foodstuff.

Let us add that a warehouse for Meat-Land will soon be established in Paris, in the large apartment house at the corner of rue des Martyrs and the boulevard Saint-Michel.

A society is being formed to market this unique substance.

We shall return to this subject.

ARFLED

Only five or six years ago, I was far from the brilliant position I have now attained, due much more, by the way, to my merit—despite what imbeciles may say—than to women. At that time, quite humble was my dress, insufficient my resources, indelicate at times my *modi vivendi*, chimerical my furnishings, illusory my credit.

I lived then in a furnished hotel, the Three-Hemispheres Hotel, situated at the top of the rue des Victimes.

The clientele of this establishment was recruited principally from every circus and music hall in the entire universe.

I met India Rubber Men from Chicago, tenors from Toulouse, clowns from Dublin, and even a lady snake charmer from Chatou.

I adored the manager's wife; she was, moreover, an exquisite manager's wife, blonde, a bit stout, no longer very young, but still quite fresh, with eyes that only asked to laugh.

I was much less fond of her husband, and, in a word, detested him.

I shared that opinion with Arfled.

Arfled? Who's Arfled? What, you don't know Arfled?

English, a very handsome lad, flexible and strong, exquisitely refined, incomplete mastery of the French language, but what does that matter when one can use mimicry?

Social situation: clown at the Fernando circus.

"Arfled," I said to him one day, "what a funny name you have!"

And he told me that, in the beginning, his name was Alfred, but one day, after cutting the letters of his name from a piece of cloth to attach to his costume, the woman entrusted with the work mistook their arrangement, and sewed them on as: Arfled.

He liked the new name very much, and kept it.

Oh, no! Arfled did not like M. Pionce, the manager of the Three-Hemispheres.

Why? I cannot be sure, but I have my suspicions.

The affection that he could have expressed for the Pionce family was concentrated, I suppose, entirely and exclusively on Madame Pionce.

Arfled was a man of taste, that's all.

Twice a day, Arfled provided, for the lovely Madame Pionce, unlimited amusement.

In the morning, he came downstairs to return his key to the desk.

If Madame Pionce happened to be alone, there passed

across Arfled's entire face an ecstatic enchantment. His eyes reflected the azure of the seventh heaven. His mouth curled up in a tight smile, like someone who has just smelled an intoxicating aroma.

And his compliments:

"Hewwo, Madaaame Pionnce, haow awe yoou? Did yoou sweep weww? Never, Madaaame Pionnce, have yoou wooked pwettier than todaaay. Gooodbye, Madaaame Pionnce, bonnne appetiiite!"

If, at the time of his descent, M. Pionce was there, Arfled assumed the expression of a fierce mastiff. He turned up his coat collar, pulled his hat over his eyes, and growled like a surly bulldog.

In the evening, exact repetition of the scenes above, according to whether M. Pionce was there or not.

So much so, that on simply seeing Arfled, Madame Pionce swooned with laughter.

One morning, Arfled found Madame Pionce in conversation with another guest.

"And M. Pionce," the man asked, "how is he?"

"No better, I'm going to send for a doctor."

Arfled's features convulsed, and in a tone of the deepest despair, he inquired:

"M. Pionnce isn't siiick, is heee?"

"Why yes, Monsieur Arfled, he was coughing all night…"

"Aaall niiight! Aoh! Aoh! The poooow fewwooow!"

And in the evening, Arfled asked about M. Pionce's cold with touching solicitude.

"Thank you, he's a little better."

Arfled clasped his hands, lifted his eyes to heaven:

"Aoh! Thaaank yoou, God, thaaank yoou!"

Unfortunately, the better did not last. The next day, relapse, vesicants.

Arfled almost fainted.

In the evening, some improvement.

Arfled fell to his knees in the office and intoned a hymn of thanksgiving:

"Thaaanks, Deeeah God, thaaanks!"

Despite her anxiety and distress, poor Madame Pionce, delighted with this comedy, doubled over with laughter.

And so the week passed, alternating between better and worse.

One evening, Arfled returned.

Madame Pionce was in the hotel office, surrounded by a few people filled with sympathy.

Her drawn features, her red eyes, indicated that it was not going well, and that perhaps it was all over.

But at the sight of Arfled, at the thought of the face he would make when he heard the fatal news, Madame Pionce forgot everything.

She fell back in her chair, overcome with laughter.

And it was only after five convulsive minutes that she could finally tell him, in a voice still interrupted by bursts of hilarity:

"He… is… dead!"

THE FORGOTTEN PIPE

A young English engineer told me, this very morning, a short and very amusing story firmly establishing the incontestable superiority of tele-electric communication over the old messengers on horseback, and even over the Chappe system, admittedly so ingenious.

On a street in London (whose name I can give you, if you insist) there are two telegraph offices, one for the London-Paris cable (via Douvres and Calais), the other for the London-Brussels cable (via Ostende). The two offices are situated facing one another, and the employees of both get along together famously. They visit one another, exchange ingenious or pleasant remarks, discuss in turn "aestheticism" or "professionalism" according to the events of the day, or their frame of mind at the moment.

Now, it happened recently that an employee of the Belgian office forgot his pipe on the desk of one of his colleagues across the street.

Quite politely, he asked a young office boy to go ask for this implement. Categorical refusal on the part of the young boy, who claimed to be there solely for the needs of the office, and not "for looking for forgotten pipes."

Coolly, the employee did not insist. He sat down to his apparatus, and asked Douvres to put him in communication with Paris, then Paris to put him in communication with Brussels, then Brussels to put him in communication with Ostende, then Ostende to put him in communication with London.

It was precisely the colleague with whom he had just been chatting who happened to be at the apparatus.

"I forgot my pipe on your deak, could you send it back by one of your boys. The only office boy available at my office refuses the errand."

Thirty seconds had not passed before the pipe, requested in this way across an important part of Europe, had returned to its proprietor.

A WHITE NIGHT FOR A RED HUSSAR

Monologue for Cadet

I've always wondered why we call a night spent out of bed a white night. I just spent a night like that, and was rather... blue.

Which did not prevent my concierge, when I returned in the morning, from greeting me with a certain expression... as if to say:

"Aha, you rascal! Taking life easy, eh?"

And yet... But I'm getting ahead of myself.

I must tell you that for some time I had been in love.

Oh, in love, you know!... not to die for. But still, lightly smitten.

She was a very sweet little blonde, with little curls all over her forehead. She was always at the window when I passed.

After I'd passed a number of times, I ended by believing that she recognized me, and gave her a little smile. I even imagined—you know how we get these ideas—that she smiled back.

That was a mistake; I had proof of that later, unfortunately too late.

I said to myself, "I'll have to look into this, some day."

While waiting, I gathered information, discreetly, without seeming to.

She was married to a rather disagreeable man, apparently, the director of a large factory that made machine-guns.

The disagreeable man went out every evening at about eight, visited his club, and didn't return until late.

"Good," I said to myself, "that's all I need."

It was then around the time of Carnival.

On the occasion of this celebration, my friends had invited me to a ball—costumed, naturally.

I'm known for my imagination; so my friends said, "Try to find an amusing costume."

And so I disguised myself, that morning, as *a red hussar from Monaco*.

You may say that there are no red hussars in Monaco, that there are no hussars there at all; or that, if there are, they generally wear street clothes.

I know that as well as you; but doesn't a bit of fantasy excuse all inexactitude?

As I contemplated myself in the wardrobe mirror (my wardrobe has a mirror), I said to myself, "Say, this would be the perfect occasion to go see my little blonde. She could never refuse such a dashing red hussar."

The fact is, just between us, that I looked pretty good in that costume. Not bad at all, in fact.

I eat early... A good dinner, substantial, to give me strength, and generously fortified with wine, to give me... nerve.

I buckle my scabbard, for I have a sword, as is only right, and there I am ready for battle.

As I approach the house of my beloved, I see the husband leave.

Good, it's going well... After he's gone a bit further, I mount the stairs, quietly, because of the spurs that I'm not quite used to, and which red hussars wear rather long.

I pull the foot of a poor doe that now serves as a bell-pull.

A footstep is heard behind the door. The door opens... There she is... my little blonde. I say to her: ....

In fact, what could I have said to her?

Because, you know, in such moments, you say whatever pops into your head, and then, five minutes later, you'll be hanged if you can repeat it.

But what I do remember perfectly is what she answered, in a furious tone: "You're mad, sir!... And my husband is coming back... I hear him now."

And bang! She slams the door in my face.

In fact, someone was indeed climbing the stairs with a heavy step, the terrible step of the pitiless husband.

As much of a red hussar as I was, I'll admit that I was nervous.

There was a simple way to resolve the situation, you'll tell me. Just go down the stairs and leave, that's all. But, as an

English philosopher once wisely observed, the simplest ideas come last.

I thought of everything, except leaving.

For a moment, I thought that I should draw my sword, and resolutely await the husband.

"Absurd," I said to myself, "and compromising."

And the man kept climbing the stairs.

All of a sudden, I see a little door, which I hadn't noticed at first because it was painted to look like marble, like the rest of the hall. But what funny marble! Real Carnival marble!

At a moment like that, there's no time to waste on frivolous esthetics.

I open the door, and rush in desperately, without even noticing where I was.

Just in time! The husband was at the top of the stairs.

I hear the grinding of a key in a lock, a door opening, a door closing—probably the same one—and finally I can breathe.

Only then do I think of examining the room that had been my salvation.

You will never guess the curious place into which I'd stuffed myself.

You smile... so you've guessed!

Yes, it was there... or rather, HERE!

Gently, without a sound, I lift the latch and push the door... It resists.

I push a little harder... It still resists.

I push very hard, with superhuman force. The door still resists, like a door that has serious reasons not to open.

I say to myself, "The wood is swollen from the humidity." I brace myself against the... thing there, and... ugh! A wasted effort.

This is, decidedly, some solid carpentry.

An infernal idea crosses my mind... What if the husband, seeing me from below, and guessing my wicked plans, had shut me in there, thanks to a lock on the outside!

What a situation for a red hussar!

On a Carnival night! And I'm expected at the ball!

No, no, it's not possible. I dismiss this sinister thought.

And yet the door remains as unmovable as a rock.

Tired of the struggle, I sit down—fortunately, you can sit in such places—and wait. Damn! Someone will soon come to my rescue.

They don't come quickly. In fact, they don't come at all.

What then do they eat in this building?

Quince jelly, I suppose.

From the street, there rise to my ears the joyful clamor of trumpets, hunting horns, bugles, and then—terrible!—the sound of clocks, every quarter hour, every half hour, every hour...!

And my anticipated liberator doesn't come. Did everyone gorge himself on bismuth that day?

The next time I visit this building, I'll send every tenant a melon.

From time to time, with touching despair, I stand up, and, calling upon all my strength, I push the door, I push, I push!

Ah! For a strong door, it's a good strong door!

Finally, exhausted, I give up. The handle of my sword is digging into my ribs. I hang it on the latch and fall asleep. A restless sleep, punctuated with nightmares. The sounds from the street die down, bit by bit. I hear only a single stubborn horn, calling heroically in the distance.

Then the horn goes to bed, like everyone else...

. . . .

I awake!... It's already early morning. I rub my eyes, and remember everything. My red hussar's heart leaps to my mouth. In a rage, I unhook my sword and pull it to me...

. . . .

I dare not tell you the rest.

What an imbecile I was! Double imbecile! Triple imbecile! Hundredfold idiot! Thousandfold cretin! I had spent the night pushing the door...

It opened inward!

BLACK CHRISTMAS

I

PROLOGUE

I would still like, in spite of my extreme lassitude, in spite of my disgust with everything going on at the moment, depite a thousand disappointments of all kinds, I would like to tell you a Christmas story.

Yes, but not a Christmas story like all the others.

In the usual Christmas stories, snow is falling, as if the Good Lord were plucking his cherubs.

If it's not snowing, in Christmas stories, at least the ground is hardened by the cold, and the heels of passers-by ring joyfully on the cobblestones.

In my Christmas story this year, if you don't mind, we will enjoy a devil of a heatwave, a scarcely astonishing phenomenon when you learn that the thing happens on a plantation in Havana.

II

A NEGRO'S DREAM

Mathias, a superb Negro of Kaffrarian origin, about twenty years old (maybe a little older, but not much) stretches out on his mat, in a corner of his hut, and dreams melancholically.

Tomorrow is Christmas, and all the legends concerning this divine day sing in his head and in his heart.

Mathias is a superb Negro, but he is a solitary Negro with sorrow in his soul.

Then, a torpor overcomes his senses, and he dreams.

His shoes, which he has placed by the chimney (in his dream, of course, for his hut contains only a small inexpensive stove of American manufacture), take on exaggerated proportions.

His shoes also change their form, and tend to take on the appearance of a gondola.

Then the gondola begins to sail on some kind of lake of love, and he is the one who steers it, he Mathias.

Behind, a fine mist envelopes like a veil… a woman, perhaps?

Yes, a woman!

A little breath of a zephyr dissipates the mist, which the waters of the lake absorb, and Mathias cries out.

The woman is the woman he loves.

III
THE BEAUTIFUL QUADROON

Imagine a block of porphry like light café au lait, rosy here and there.

Cut from this block the robust and sensual statue of a young woman of sixteen.

Give her incomparable black hair, eyes like brown diamonds, overly thick eyebrows that almost meet, correct the slight harshness of those eyebrows with a large mouth, like a good girl, and the turning up of a little nose that is absolutely delightful.

You have thus obtained Maria-Anna, the planter's daughter.

IV
WHAT MATHIAS WAS

Mathias was not your ordinary Negro.

Born on the plantation to former slaves turned faithful servants, his intelligence and desire to learn showed themselves at an early age.

Remarkably ingenious, he could do whatever he wanted with his fingers, and with the other parts of his body.

A chemist of the first water, he discovered how to

synthesize nicotine, by heating, in isolation, equal parts of quicklime and cow dung with two or three slices of beetroot.

Shortly after this discovery, he received an academic award in recognition of his fine work on "the use of cabbage leaves in cigars for French industry."[1]

By an adroit and considered contact between the cabbage leaf and the tobacco leaf, he promptly arrived at the remarkable result that the cabbage leaf seemed like a tobacco leaf, whereas the latter could easily have been used as an old walnut leaf.

So much so that one could have said to the Tobacco Leaf, as in the delicious fable by Saadi: "Excuse me, Mademoiselle, are you not the Tobacco Leaf?" To which the Cabbage Leaf would have replied: "No, Madame, I am not the Tobacco Leaf, but having frequently visited her, I have kept her perfume."

V

CHRISTMAS EVE

Every year, at Christmas (it was an old tradition on the plantation), el señor S. Cargo, the owner, a very handsome mulatto, convened around his table all the personnel of the hacienda.

They feasted joyfully to the health of the baby Jesus. They ate, they drank, they toasted, they talked foolishness. Those who were intemperate had the right, that night, to stuff themselves up to there, and even a bit higher.

The beautiful Maria-Anna presided, and Mathias never let her out of his sight.

Poor Mathias! His dream that day made him tingle all over, and it was twin fires that served him as eyes.

Every time the young woman's eyes met the Negro's eyes, her divine cheeks of porphyry and light café au lait blushed a little more.

In the morning, Mathias, strongly encouraged by overindulgence in fermented liquors, went to find el señor S. Cargo and said to him:

"Master, you know the man that I am."

"I know full well, my fine friend, and have but one word to say to you, the word that Mac Mahon gave to a young man of your race: continue."

"I shall continue, Master, if you give me Maria-Anna in marriage."

"You're dreaming! You, a Negro!"

And this word was pronounced in such a tone that Mathias though it best not to insist.

VI
A NEGRO'S TEARS

As soon as he had returned to his hut, Mathias collapsed onto his bed, and, for the first time in his life, this man of ebony wept.

He wept for a long time, copiously, tears of rage and depair. Then a physical lassitude overtook him, and he wanted to sleep.

A glance at his mirror drew a cry from him.

The tears coursing down his cheeks had left something like a wide white trail.

What then had happened to him?

Oh! Nothing that was not quite simple and quite explicable.

Mathias's tears, become strongly caustic by the sodium-magnesium of despair, destroyed the black pigment of his skin, and pink appeared.[2]

A ray of light!

VII

MATHIAS CONTINUES TO WEEP

Mathias carefully hid his discovery from everyone in his entourage, but every time that he had a minute, he ran to lock himself in his hut, shed tears of rage in torrents, and spread them, with a little brush, over every part of his body.

Then, to avoid suspicion, he covered them with black polish, and the world saw nothing but blue skies.

VIII
APOTHEOSIS

After several months, Mathias had become as white as Monsieur Edmond Blanc himself.

A year had passed.

Once again, it is Christmas Eve. All of the personnel can be found gathered around the table presided over by S. Cargo and his delicious daughter Maria-Anna.

Nobody is missing but Mathias.

Suddenly, an elegant gentleman, faultless high collar, polished pumps, violet ribbon at his lapel, enters the room.

Nobody in the company recognizes him, except Maria-Anna, who is not fooled a minute, by that look in his eyes!

"Mathias!" she cries. "I love him!"

And she faints from the emotion.

El señor S. Cargo had no more objection to raise against the marriage of the two young people.

The wedding soon took place.

And they had many children, so many children that they soon gave up trying to count them.

1. Cigars do not grow on trees, as many persons wrongly imagine. It is, on the contrary, a manufactured product whose fabrication demands a great deal of tact and expertise.

2. Some ignorant people might be surprised that tears caustic enough to destroy black would respect pink. Because, you pack of animals, the pink coloration of the skin is not due to a pigment, but to the blood that you see by transparency.

ONE FOR TOMORROW

She is six years old.

In her pretty and delicate face, there is barely enough room for her large pale periwinkle eyes, the poor suffering eyes of a young woman who loves too much.

She seems like an exquisite and wildly expensive bibelot, a rare and disturbing bibelot.

Often, she is playful and happy, like other girls her age, and then at times, for no reason, she stops laughing to stare at nothing, fixedly, far off.

When spoken to, she says anything at all, in such a funny voice.

Sunday, we were amusing ourselves by asking the children about their little flirtations.

"And you, Jeannette, who will you marry when you grow up?"

"I'll marry Georges."

"Who is Georges?"

"He's a little boy we play with on the Champs-Elysées."

"Is he nice?"

"Oh, no! He's even very ugly, with his red hair and his nasty big nose."

"Is he rich, then?"

"I don't think so, because he has patches on the sleeve of his coat."

"Why then?"

She waits a full minute before answering. A long voluptuous shudder passes through her little shoulders, and, gazing into the distance, she says in a voice like a somnambulist:

"Oh! I like it so much when he kisses me!"

A LUMINOUS IDEA

This morning, I received a visit from an amusing character... an inventor!

Do you like inventors? Me, I adore them, even if they don't invent anything, which is the case with practically all inventors.

I like their obsession, the fire in their eyes, their disheveled appearance. As for obsession and fire in the eyes, my man was in the grand tradition, but it was especially in the matter of slovenly attire that he exceeded all that I'd seen before.

In particular, a button on his coat inserted, as if by chance, into a buttonhole on his vest, and reciprocally.

It was rather picturesque.

. . . .

I was shaving before the mirror (I shave myself, now).

The man blew in like a hurricane.

"Hello," he said. "How are you?"

"No worse than yesterday," I replied. "And yourself?"

"Do you recognize me?"

"Me? Not at all."

"Ah! I was about to say, it's because I have a beard now... And besides, you've never seen me before."

Without reminding the man that, strictly speaking, the second reason sufficed, I asked the object of his visit.

"I am an inventor, sir," he answered proudly.

"Ah! Heavens, I'd already guessed."

"I come to you because you are a man who is intelligent, well educated, and cares nothing for money, where a good idea is concerned."

I bowed.

I am, in fact, intelligent and well educated; and when an idea strikes me as practical, ingenious, or simply bizarre, I will not hesitate to sacrifice a million or two to realize it.

Brusquely, the man continued:

"Which do you prefer... to burn or to rot?"

"Excuse me," I said, a bit startled, "to rot?"

"Or to burn. Well, answer me."

"My God, sir, the idea of rotting is in no way particularly seductive. As for burning, may I confess that I am not irresistibly drawn to it, at the moment?"

"At the moment, yes, but when you're dead?"

"Oh! When I'm dead!"

And I sketched a gesture of utter indifference.

My inventor continued, in a rather vulgar tone:

"Yes, rotting in the ground is really disgusting, but being burned isn't much nicer."

"However..."

"There is no however. I have invented a process that

makes cremation and burial obsolete. I replace all that with *inaeration*! Eh? *Inaeration!*

"That's not a foolish idea."

"Don't mock me before you learn more."

"I assure you, sir..."

"Drop it. You're dead, right?"

"Just a minute!"

"It's just a supposition. You're dead, they bring me your body, I put it in my oven..."

"But that's cremation."

"Imbecile! I put it in my oven, a special oven of my own invention, and I desiccate it. I desiccate it. Do you understand? I DESICCATE it. I do not cook it, I do not roast it, I do not burn it, I DES-IC-CATE IT. That is to say that I rid it of all the water that it contains by evaporation... Do you know the approximate proportion of water in the human body?"

"I admit that I..."

"Well, it's about eighty per cent, four fifths."

"That much?"

"Yes sir, that much. So General Boulanger, whom you worship so..."

"But I never said..."

"Don't interrupt... General Boulanger, whom you worship so, weighs eighty-two kilograms; therefore he represents roughly sixty-five kilograms of water. So, for every eighty-two times that you cry 'Hooray for Boulanger,' you should count sixty-five for pure water. So much for human importance! And Francisque Sarcey, then! Do you know Sarcey?"

"I know him without knowing him. Sometimes in the morning, as I walk along rue de Douai, I see him shaking a scatter rug out the window, but you can't call that knowing a man."

"Well, it's frightening how much water Sarcey contains. I can't give you the exact number, you'd think I was joking. On the other hand, there are some individuals who offer very little excess. Sarah Bernhardt, for example, there's a temperament that's truly... What's the word?"

"Dramatic?"

"No, *anhydrous*."

"Materialist!"

"Are you married?"

"Not at the moment."

"Do you have a mistress?"

"Mistress would be an exaggeration, but I have a sweet little girlfriend."

"How much does she weigh?"

"My word, I never weighed her, but I can tell you approximately... Let's see, she's not too big, probably about fifty kilos."

"Well, let me tell you that the object of your idolatry contains about forty kilos of water."

"Stop it, you disgust me!"

"Forty liters of water! You hear me... *eighty pints!*"

And the inventor pronounced the words "eighty pints" in a tone of indescribable contempt. And what had I ever done to him?

He continued point-blank:

"But you're just wasting my time with this business about your girlfriend. Let me return to my invention: Once your body is entirely desiccated, I soak it in a liquid of my own composition, based on nitric acid, which transforms it into an explosive material similar to guncotton. Then, all you do is ignite it... Pfff... fff... ttt! A flash of light, a great cloud of white smoke rises to the sky, and all is said and done! What do you think of my idea?"

"It's luminous."

"But that's not all. Instead of transforming your body into a simple explosive, I can create a complete fireworks display: firecrackers, Roman candles, rockets, Catherine wheels, etc., etc. For poor families, I can transform, for only thirty francs, the dear departed into Roman candles of all colors. For ten thousand francs, I can produce a first-class display with an allegorical bouquet."

"Superb!"

"Better yet... Old soldiers could will their mortal remains, transformed in this way, to the artillery. They could be loaded into shells or cannons. What a joy, ten years after your death, to shoot the enemies of France! Doesn't that tempt you?"

"Yes, it's an inviting proposition, but as far as my personal body is concerned, I prefer to wait."

The inventor took his hat and stormed out, furious.

What do you want? I'm in no hurry.

SUGGESTION

Just then, Captain Cap felt the need to assume an air of mystery. And, as a glimmer of curiosity kindled in our eyes:

"Don't blame me," the Captain said, "I can say no more. My ORDER prohibits it."

Captain Cap belongs to a quite extraordinary Order, whose usefulness is second to none.

Offered any proposition to which he has the slightest objection, Captain Cap coldly protests:

"I am very sorry, my dear chap, but my Order prohibits it!"

And he adds with that smile that is his alone:

"Don't blame me."

Nevertheless and all the same, Cap was burning to speak.

We pretended to busy ourselves with other matters, and soon the Captain said:

"An amazing subject!"

Solely so that we might hear the rest of the story, none of us batted an eyelid.

"Imagine," Cap persisted.

Bored did we appear to this insistence.

Then Cap opened the sluices.

It concerned an amazing little lady. You could hypnotize her like that, one, two! And there you were! An amazing subject, I tell you!

Once asleep, she was nothing but soft wax between the fingers of your will.

If we liked, we could go that very evening.

We went.

With the rough hand of a seasoned mariner, Cap took the tiny hands of the little Montmartrian shepherdess.

One, two, three... She is asleep.

Then Cap pulled from his pocket a raw potato and a guava.

Having peeled both, he offered the subject a slice of raw potato, saying in a loud voice trembling with suggestion:

"Eat this, it is guava."

No sooner had the child chewed a piece of the tuber, when she expressed strong disgust. She even spat it out, grimacing like the devil.

A smile on his lips, Cap changed the experiment.

This time it was guava that he gave the young lady, saying in a voice of no less authority:

"Eat this, it is a raw potato."

No sooner had the child chewed a morsel of the fruit, when she asked for more.

She finished off the whole guava.

As we left the house, the Captain said, with lively scientific interest:

"A curious case, eh, the depravity of that girl, who adores raw potato, but can't taste guava?"

ABSINTHES

Five o'clock...

Nasty weather... gray... a hellish dirty melancholy gray...

How about a good downpour to flush away all of these morons who strut around looking stupid!... Nasty weather...

A bad day today, damn it!... Bad luck...

Article rejected... politely.

"Your article is very good... interesting subject... well written, but... not really in the spirit of the paper."

The spirit of the paper!... Oh. the beautiful spirit of the paper!... the stupidest paper in Paris and Seine-et-Oise!

A busy and distracted editor:

"Give the gentleman back his manuscript... Your novel is very good... interesting subject... well written, but you understand... business is bad... such a backlog... and besides, couldn't you do something more like *The Marl-Pit Mystery*? That would sell... maybe win an award."

Walked out looking friendly and foolish:

"Maybe some other time..."

Nasty weather... five thirty...

The boulevard!... Let's take the boulevard... maybe I'll meet some friends... Wonderful friends!... Swine, all of them... Can't you count on anyone in Paris?

All these people are so ugly!

And the women so poorly dressed!... And the men look like idiots!

"Waiter... an absinthe with sugar!"

It's amusing, the sugar cube melting so nicely on its little spoon... Like granite worn away by dripping water... except that sugar isn't as hard as granite... Fortunately... could you imagine that: absinthe with granite?

Absinthe with granite... ha ha ha ha... ha ha ha... Pretty funny... absinthe with granite... better not be in a hurry... ha ha ha...

The sugar is almost melted now... We're a lot like that... The sugar cube is a striking symbol of mankind...

Once we're dead, we'll wear away like that... atom by atom... molecule by molecule... dissolved, decayed, returned to the Great Everything by the gracious intervention of plants and earthworms.

We'll be happier then... Victor Hugo and Anatole Beaucanard equal before the Maggot... Fortunately!

Nasty weather... Bad day... Stupid editor... Even stupider publisher.

And then... maybe I'm not so talented after all, really.

Good stuff, absinthe... not the first sip, but after that.

It's good.

Six o'clock... The boulevard is starting to pick up... A good time for the ladies!

Prettier than before... and more elegant! And the men don't look so stupid!

The sky is still gray... a lovely pearl gray... refined... in good taste... The setting sun tints the clouds with lovely pale copper blushes... And it's very nice...

"Waiter... an absinthe with anisette!"

Absinthe with sugar is amusing, but hell... it takes too long.

Six thirty...

Look at all those women!... Most of them pretty... and strange, too!

And mysterious!

Where do they come from?... Where do they go?... Will we ever know?...

They barely look at me... I who love them so!

Each one, as she passes, is so striking that I'm sure I'll never forget her... and as soon as she's gone I can't even remember what she looked like.

Fortunately, the next ones are even better.

I would love them so much if they wanted... But they pass on by... Will I ever see them again?

On the sidewalk in front of me, men selling everything... newspapers... celluloid cigar cases... little stuffed monkeys... in all colors...

Who are these men? Beaten down by life, probably... unrecognized geniuses... rebels... How deep their eyes are...

What dark fire in their pupils!...

There's a book to be done about all that... unique... unforgettable... a book everyone will have to buy... everyone!

Oh! All those women!...

Why doesn't one of them come over and sit by me, and kiss me sweetly... and caress me... and rock me like my mama did when I was little?...

"Waiter... straight absinthe... And don't be afraid to fill it up."

THE PARROT

"You'll see, that little troublemaker will make us miss the train again!"

This imprecation offered in the middle of the Havre station[1] (departures) was immediately followed by the arrival of a car carrying the little troublemaker in question.

Not alone, the young lady. A sailor accompanied her, a rough man of the sea, who held, in his bronzed hands, a parrot installed in an enormous cage, a cage in which an adult lion could have sported at his ease.

"What's all this about?" I asked, rather discourteously.

And my little friend replied in her disarming warble:

"You'll probably scold me, my dear, but too bad!… It's too good an opportunity!"

The good opportunity consisted in having acquired, for the paltry sum of 15 louis, a parrot that would have cost all of 40 francs on the quai de la Mégisserie, a stupid and nasty parrot, that howled like a polecat, without articulating anything that resembled organized speech.

"You see how well he talks?" asked my companion, to worsen matters.

During this little family scene, the intrepid navigator

seemed a bit annoyed.

"This man brought it back himself from Brazil," the child continued to warble.

I immediately recognized the parrot merchant, who was none other than a sailor from the François I (Le Havre-Trouville), on leave at the moment, due to the choleriform suspension of service.

"You just arrived from Brazil?" I asked sarcastically.

"Not directly, but a friend..."

"And that bird is worth 300 francs?"

"Oh, my God! I said 300 francs like I would have said anything."

"Well then! You can send it back to Brazil, that Pretty Polly of yours, there are enough animals in the house as it is!"

My young friend, seeing that she was in the wrong, decided to fly into a rage.

"Is that me you're talking about?"

I have never hurt a woman, even with a flower. So I replied sweetly:

"You silly goose!"

And I slipped into the boatman's hand a 50 franc note, which he must have mistaken for a bill of five louis, for he hurried away, his beret in his hand, and visibly enchanted.

It was no small affair to install the chattering bird in the compartment. It would have been easier, I think, to introduce the car into the cage than the cage into the car.

Finally, thanks to the kindness of an old decorated gentlemen, who responded to my Jane's big eyes with a swinish squint, we achieved a sort of almost acceptable heap.

The exit was harder. We came close to having to remove the roof from the train.

And that pig of a parrot who never stopped screeching its hoarse and inarticulate cries!

The people in the train were enormously amused, and the employees were not bored. Me, I was half as white as a sheet, from fury, and red as a rooster, from rage!

As for Jane, she had thought it prudent to absent herself momentarily, on the pretext of looking for a car.

The return to the house was stormy. But I'm so nice! A couple of slaps, and I'm no longer mad at anyone. I'm even accused of being too nice.

In short, that damned parrot was no worse than any other.

Without his unbearable clamor, he would have been a charming bird.

His green feathers that fell, rich and thick, to his ankles (or at least to whatever parrots use as ankles) gave him the amusing appearance of a suave dandy.

On his head he had a red plume, which he seemed proud of to the point of impertinence.

And his little round eyes, which he winked so maliciously, the idiot!

And besides, Jane loved him so much that I ended by getting used to him.

As for his stubborn refusal to ever parody, or even sound like, human speech, my beloved attributed that inferiority to shyness.

"Goodness!" she said. "The way you always look so mad at him, the poor little thing, he's afraid to say anything."

The idea of owning a timid parrot delighted my soul to a degree that I cannot express.

I decided to come to terms with the situation, and, yesterday, I offered this proposition:

"What do you think, if we got him a little drunk, maybe that would loosen his tongue?"

"We can always try," Jane gravely replied.

At first, the poor animal refused to swallow the champagne.

The little bubbles of carbonic acid tickled his nostrils (do birds have nostrils?), then, gradually, he developed a taste for the drink, and consumed more of it than was reasonable.

Then, it was epic.

That parrot was as drunk as a skunk: he staggered, fell, and picked himself up to tumble anew.

His beautiful red plume had slipped over his right ear; his little eyes winked with a funny sparkle.

And then, all at once he started to sing, in a piercing voice, the well-known refrain:

> I got a skinful
> Coming back from Suresnes!

1. Not the Saint-Lazare station, as the superficial reader might be tempted to believe, but the Havre-De-Grâce station.

FORGETFULNESS

I met her in a restaurant.

For some time she had been coming regularly, every evening at six o'clock. To my despair, she paid no attention to my person.

In vain had I installed myself at a nearby table, given myself a pleasant expression, done for her those little services that one does between customers; nothing worked.

However, one day when she was becoming impatient knocking on the table, without getting the waiter's attention, I summoned my most indignant voice, and thundered:

"Are you deaf, waiter? Madame has been calling you for two hours!"

She turned to me and thanked me with a smile.

I fell in love with her immediately.

On her side, the ice had been broken.

From that moment on, she never failed to say good evening every day when she entered, a pretty little "good evening" that was as gracious and stylish as herself.

And then we became good friends.

Her name was Lucienne.

Without being an "honest woman," she was no "cocotte"

either. She belonged to that category of young women whom the bourgeois stigmatize as "kept women."

Her "monsieur," a large man of extraordinary dignity, visited her only rarely. Inspector with a company for insurance against poisonous mushrooms, he often traveled in the provinces, and left Lucienne at her leisure.

The only inconvenience to this liaison was that the man was terribly jealous, and that he always arrived at the lady's place unannounced, when she least expected him.

Without showing a violent passion for me, Lucienne was fond of me.

At the time, I was still young, and titulary of a joyful disposition, which the torments of life have now swept away like a broom of straw.

Lucienne was also quite cheerful.

Me, I had fallen madly in love with her, and for several days had not concealed my flame from her.

She laughed loudly at my declarations, and repeated to me, "One of these days... One of these days!" But "one of these days" was not arriving soon enough for my taste.

One evening, I timidly offered to take her to the theater. My friend Paul Lordon, then secretary of the Porte-Saint-Martin, had offered me two seats to I forget which play.

She accepted.

After the performance, in the car that brought us back, she finally let herself be swayed by my supplications, and decided this: She would first go up to her place to verify that the dignified man was not previously installed, in which case I had only to retire. If the place was free, she would give me the signal, by placing in her bedroom window a lamp fitted with a scarlet lampshade.

It was raining in torrents.

Panting with desire, I waited on the sidewalk facing the luminous signal.

Minutes passed, then quarters of hours. Not the slightest red gleam. Despair in my heart, and soaked to the marrow, I decided to return home.

Ah! If in that moment, I had taken hold of "monsieur," I would have made him forget his dignity!

The next day, I was greeted more than coldly by Lucienne.

"You're a nice one, you!" she told me in a tone as harsh as flint.

And, as I assumed my most stunned expression, she continued:

"I waited for you all night…"

"But the lamp…"

"The lamp? I put it in the window right away, as soon as I arrived."

"I swear to you that I stayed at least an hour on the sidewalk across the street, and I saw nothing."

"Do you have molasses in your eyes?"

"I swear it…"

"Leave me alone!"

And she installed herself, furious, before her tapioca.

I must have looked very stupid.

And then, suddenly, there she is dropping her spoon and falling back in her chair, gripped by a tumultuous and prolonged burst of laughter, interrupted by the occasional "Oh, my God! How funny!"

Gradually, her joyous spasm diminished in intensity, but not enough to let her explain.

She turned to me with a friendly look, wet with tears of laughter, and totally reconciled:

"Ah, my poor friend! Just imagine that I forgot…"

And the laughter began again.

"What?" I asked. "To light your lamp, perhaps?"

"No, that's not it…"

She made an effort and could finally speak.

"I forgot that my bedroom window looks out on the courtyard."

AN UNFORTUNATE

I no longer remember the name of the poet who proclaimed: "Ah! It is a noble task to help one's neighbor!" How right he was!

The forms of charity are multiple, like the forms of human misery. One of the most agreeable is that which consists of doing good around oneself without spending an obol, a penny, a red farthing.

And it is not one of the least benefits of our noble profession of columnist, that we can interest our friend the public in the dismaying misfortunes that enamel our epoch, and that without opening our wallet. On the contrary, even, it is copy already written. For (why deny it?) we live in a very singular epoch. *O tempora! O mores!* (and his friends).

So it was that, this very morning, I received a letter that broke my heart like firewood.

The poor boy who wrote me this sorrowful missive gives me details that are scarcely credible, and which inculcate in you a pretty idea of the society in which we are forced to live.

He is almost 28. A former inspector for the "General Insurance Company Against Notaries in Southern France," he now finds himself with no other support than a miserable monthly pension of twenty-five louis given by his father, a former miller in the North, now retired from business.

Unfortunately, he is not alone.

His companion, a young woman whom he married in the face of nature, without passing through the indecent formalities of city hall or the church, has given him a baby twenty months old. (That is to say, the baby is now twenty months old, but when it was born, it was no older than other children of the same age.)

And this whole little world swarms through an apartment costing 1800 francs (before taxes), devoid of all that gives life its charm.

Enough, you say. It is too sad.

And what does the poor boy ask? Money? Oh, far from it!

Some occupation suited to his abilities.

He is not lacking for ideas. Listen to him, rather, and if there are any backers to be found among the readership, may they rest assured that they will, at the same time, do a good deed and excellent business.

"What would you say, for example, of organizing a tour for His Holiness Pope Leo XIII through Europe and America? The Sovereign Pontiff should be modern like everyone else. What popularity wouldn't he achieve by exhibiting himself everywhere? etc., etc."

Follows the development of the plan, organization of the tour, itinerary, so much percentage for the impresario, so much percentage for the "Peter's Pence," etc.

You have there an excellent idea to consider, and gold to pick up as with a shovel.

And the unfortunate young man concludes his letter with this:

"In case my idea meets with no enthusiasts, could you possibly, with your connections, procure me a place as an interpreter for a Belgian family spending the winter in the South? These people, of course, must speak neither the Walloon dialect, which I don't know, nor Flemish, which I don't understand at all."

I sincerely hope that the supreme call of this Desperate Man will not fall solely on ears of stone.

It is up to the backers or the Belgians.

A WILL

Quite recently, a wealthy landowner died in a little town in the center, which I cannot, to my great regret, specify (my space here being limited, rigorously).

When alive, this fine man had been a mighty lover before the Lord. Not a girl, not a woman of the region could boast of having escaped this indefatigable skirt chaser.

His generosity, let us add quickly, equalled his ardor, and this man who was known for pinching anatomies did not extend that behavior to pennies.

His death put the whole region into mourning.

As soon as he had passed, his heirs opened his will, and this is what they read:

"I want to be neither buried nor incinerated.

"Forty-eight hours after my demise, place my body in a big pot with water, and boil it until it is completely cooked.

"The meat and broth will be distributed to my pigs.

"(Having, all my life, lived as a pig, it is fitting that I end in a pig.)

"As for my skeleton, it is to undergo the process used in industry to extract phosphorus from bones.

"This phosphorus, divided into little pieces, will

be distributed in little lamps analogous to those that, sempiternally, burn before tabernacles.

"(I burned the candle at both ends, throughout my life, and it would be a cruel privation not to provide a bit more light, after my death.)"

Well! This will, so sincere, so logical, could not be executed, the Authorities being formally opposed to it.

How, I ask you, would it have upset the Authorities if a wealthy landowner in the center of France had been boiled rather than burned?

And besides, what business is it of theirs?

LOVE AMONG SYRIAN TORTOISES

I do not have the honor of knowing M. de Cherville, but I like him very much.

It is he who brings, to M. Hébrard's austere *Temps*, something like a breath of fresh air, something like a good whiff of the farm and garden.

It is he who comes to announce, in our forgetful Paris, that the canola looks promising, that we will have a good half year for barley; unfortunately, as far as buckwheat is concerned, the harvest will be practically null, except in the Orne and the Ille-et-Villaine.

Anecdotes often enliven these rural technicalities, and also childhood memories dear to M. de Cherville. He remembers the fine cherries that he devoured one day, with a pretty little cousin, in the shade of a *Magnolia grandiflora*, which, too, has its story.

Only one thing sullies my respectful esteem for M. de Cherville, and that is the terrible hatred that he professes for poachers. (Me, I'm for the poachers.)

M. de Cherville considers "game" as a sort of extremely special entity, organized by the Creator for the exclusive amusement and alimentation of the wealthy.

The peasant who fricassees a rabbit caught in the alfafa seems, to M. de Cherville, to deserve the blackest of punishments.

Despite his talent and wit, M. de Cherville has the weakness to believe in the ruling class.

There is on this matter, between M. de Cherville and me, a slight divergence of opinion upon which I will have the good taste not to insist.

Be that as it may, M. de Cherville knows some fine stories about the animals, and he tells them marvelously.

He knows their customs and their romances. There is not an alcove in nature in which this amiable voyeur has not drilled his hole!

So, the tortoises! Do you know how tortoises love in Syria?

If it's true, as is said, that love is nothing but the contact of two epidermises, the poor tortoises could only enjoy very limited pleasures. Well! Strike that notion from your copybook, and read M. de Cherville:

"...In the season of love, the male tortoise pursues the female, solicits her, bedevils her, but without success; the female resists all invitations. So, the lover goes in search of a certain herb of which the female is very fond, picks it, and brings it to her. She has no sooner tasted it, than all thought of resistance vanishes, she abandons herself to her wily seducer, and for a moment, both of them rival in happiness the gods of Olympus, who surpass them only in the advantage of being able to forego the magic herb."

Huh! What do you say to that? And, instead of sending ordinary and expensive flowers to your beloved, would it not be more clever to hand her a little packet of this magic herb?

The young Syrians have thought of it:

"When a beauty proves cruel," M. de Cherville adds, "one can see, in the evening, the rejected suitor take a melancholy stroll in some glen; one might assume he hopes to soothe the bitterness of his despair: he is simply in search of a male tortoise; he has no difficulty in meeting one, as the species is plentiful in the country. Then, he follows him until he sees him pick the famous talisman, seizes it, and then makes sure to slip it into the young lady's clothing. For with our species, it is not even necessary for digestion to pass the juice of the blessed herb into the subject's organism for it to produce its effect."

The name of the herb, Monsieur de Cherville!… For pity's sake, the name of the herb!

Or, failing that, I will do as the young and handsome Dunois, and leave for Syria!

THE GENTLEMAN AND THE HARDWARE CLERK
AN ENGLISH STORY

I have been, for a few days now, seeing a little English girl, not very pretty, but a lot of fun, and whose lechery is offset by the most delightful sense of humor.

The funny stories she tells me!

And with such funny expressions!

Her remarkable nerve allows her to coolly affirm that it all really happened, but I, I don't believe her.

I'm terribly afraid that the example I'm about to give will not produce the enormous impression of hilarity that I feel myself. This is probably because you won't be able to see Lucy's comical faces, or hear her twittering accent, which is both amusing and charming.

This is a dialogue between a gentleman and a hardware clerk. The gentleman enters the shop:

THE GENTLEMAN: Good day, monsieur.

THE HARDWARE CLERK: Good day, monsieur.

THE GENTLEMAN: I would like to purchase one of those devices that can be fitted onto doors, and which makes them close by themselves.

THE HARDWARE CLERK: I understand what you want, monsieur. It's a device for closing doors automatically.

THE GENTLEMAN: Precisely. I would like a system that is not too expensive.

THE HARDWARE CLERK: Yes, monsieur, an economical device for closing doors automatically.

THE GENTLEMAN: And above all, not too complicated.

THE HARDWARE CLERK: In other words, you want a simple and inexpensive device for closing doors automatically.

THE GENTLEMAN: Exactly. And also, not one of those devices that closes doors so abruptly…

THE HARDWARE CLERK: That it's like a cannon shot! I see what you need: a simple device, inexpensive, not too brutal, for closing doors automatically.

THE GENTLEMAN: That's it. But not one of those devices that closes doors so slowly…

THE HARDWARE CLERK: That you think you're going to die! The article that you desire, in short, is a simple device, inexpensive, neither too slow nor too brutal, for closing doors automatically.

THE GENTLEMAN: You understand me completely. Ah! And also my device shouldn't need, like other systems I've seen, the strength of a bull to open the door.

THE HARDWARE CLERK: Of course. Let us summarize. What you want is a simple device, inexpensive, neither too slow nor too brutal, easy to handle, for closing doors automatically.

· ·

The dialogue continues for several minutes more.

· ·

THE GENTLEMAN: Well, then! Show me a model.

THE HARDWARE CLERK: I'm sorry, monsieur, but I don't have any devices for closing doors automatically.

A GOOD SOCIETY

My little Libyan slave (a young Negress of about thirteen) brought me, on a golden platter studded with gems, the following card:

BARONESS PATAN DE ROUSPÉTANCE
PRESIDENT OF THE SOCIETY
FOR OLD WOODEN MATCHSTICKS

I ran my fine long hand through the curly opulence of my ebony locks, I sharpened the points of my victorious mustache, I fingered my muttonchops, and:

"Show the lady in," I said in my caressing voice.

Madame the Baroness Patan de Rouspétance entered the intoxicating alcove that serves as my salon.

She is a charming woman, with exquisite manners, and with an admirable understanding of a good joke, which does no harm.

"Monsieur," she began, after a brief silence and some excusable embarrassment, "I have been delegated by the ladies of the Society for Old Wooden Matchsticks to come implore you for the publicity that you alone can give our enterprise. Your universally respected name, your immense talent, the seductiveness of your person, the truly derisive sums you received for the Panama Canal, everything, in a word, everything designated you to be our spokesman to the public."

I bowed, like a violet stirred by the breeze.

"Here is the goal of our society," continued the woman… "But first, do you have any interest in statistics?"

"I am one of its incontested masters."

"Then you must be aware that each French citizen produces, on the average, every day, one gram of burned matchsticks, which makes, *grosso modo*, for all of France, 34 million grams, that is, 34 thousand kilos of wood lost daily to the world. We have decided, my dear master, to collect all of this wasted material and to use it to heat poor families. Now, with 34,000 kilos of wood a day, do you know how many poor families we could heat?"

"I have never tried the experiment."

"We could heat 34,000 of them, at the rate, of course, of 10 kilos per family, which is quite enough for active people…"

"Who stamp their feet to keep warm between meals."

"That's not all… Have you ever considered all the wood lost in the form of pencil shavings?"

"At the mere idea, madame, I cannot sleep."

"Let us say 20,000 kilos a day. More heat for 2,000 needy households!… But for that, dear master, the press must help us. The public must know our work and become impassioned."

The Baroness had at that moment one of those smiles!…

"Count on me, madame," I said, as I helped her to her feet. "Tomorrow, the great public will learn of your work, will appreciate your noble task…"

Great sobs prevented me from finishing.

And now, generous readers, and you, compassionate readeresses, you know what it remains for you to do.

For additional information, inquire at the Society's office.

THE CYCLIST

Of course, in the current of my urban, suburban, and departmental life, I've seen many dirty people. I've seen some even dirtier than that.

But I don't remember having seen any more sumptuously dirty than the cyclist who stopped before the café of Nice, where we were loafing before who knows which vermouth.

Oh, the swine! One would think he had kept his boots long submerged in unnamable swamps, which frogs had also visited, besides, to relieve themselves in every way, without a single exception.

I would like to believe that this gentleman's staff had polished his boots, that very morning, but for heaven's sake! It was not apparent.

What kilometers had he not traveled, this record holder, through what muddy hectares had he not waded!

Oh, those poor boots!

And who can ever tell the supreme happiness that he felt on contemplating how dirty he had made his expensive ankle boots!

And yet, when the little Italian shoeshine boy, with his black eyes, with his white teeth, offered to polish the glorious boots, the cyclist didn't dare refuse, and the young transalpine set to work with all his body and soul.

Despite the fact that the operation was none too interesting, all of us paid keen attention to the work.

Finally, the right boot was prepared, cleaned, polished, blackened, as shiny as the soul of the devil.

Little Crispi, joyful at his semi-triumph, was about to apply himself to the left boot, when the manager of the café appeared.

And then, the manager of the café (wearing, on one of his arms, the emblematic serviette), stretched toward the horizon his other hand (definitive), ordering the child-cleaner to depart in no uncertain terms.

The shoeshine boy fled, terrified.

The cyclist mounted his nickel-plated steed, and disappeared in the direction of Monte-Carlo, probably to try to save face.

EXTRA STORIES

THE BEAUTIFUL PORK-BUTCHER

Ever since that unfortunate incident, I cannot pass a porkbutcher without a pang in my heart and a shiver of regret.

It was in… I don't remember the year, but do you recall the coachmen's strike? It was around that time.

I had noticed her, one day when I was idling in the neighborhood of the Temple. She was enthroned behind her counter, among her hams, garlands of saveloys, and aspics that trembled whenever a bus passed.

One can truly say that she was enthroned, for she could have been taken for a queen, with her fine head, so impassive and reasonable, her ivory forehead, framed by her parted black hair. Her eyelashes, just as black, gave her enormous Junoesque eyes a troubling veil.

Her admirable face, all black and white, was cut violently by her mouth, very full and very red. The scarlet seemed to sound a fanfare of rude good health and robust sensuality.

The first time that I saw her, I was rooted before the window of the shop.

A customer entered. She rose to serve him. I saw that she was tall, and admirably formed, somewhat lanky perhaps. Standing, she looked younger than when seated. Under twenty.

The next day, having returned to wander around there, I decided to enter. The excuse was a sausage, which she served me with charming and serious grace.

And I went back every day.

I entered and bought various cold cuts, which I distributed afterwards to the little apprentices in the neighborhood.

Before her, on the marble counter, were spread the plates and terrines. I admired her marvelous skill at cutting, with a quick slice of the knife, just the right weight, a quarter kilo, or an eighth.

I had noticed that the comestible furthest from her was the boar's head with pistachios. When you requested it, she leaned over, and then you could admire her figure, as lithe as a willow. Her neck, as white as cream, stretched out, emerging from a flat collar, which looked pale next to that beautiful flesh.

It was always boar's head with pistachios that I wanted. And often, to see a bit more of her neck, I moved the platter away from her, while she served another customer.

One time, I even moved the boar's head to the edge of the counter. She was obliged to lean over and stretch her neck far forward, so far that I glimpsed a maddening little black mole, a fly in the milk.

One day, I no longer dared return to her shop (true lovers sometimes have these sudden spells of timidity).

I contented myself with passing and repassing by outside.

And then I no longer dared even pass by.

It seemed to me that the people in the area, and the policemen, had noticed me and were pointing at me.

One morning—I shall always remember that it was a Sunday morning—I had a brilliant idea.

The coachmen having just gone on strike, the companies had called for young men who were unemployed and could handle a horse to replace the strikers.

I presented myself.

After a perfunctory test, I was entrusted with a hackney coach that seemed like an old emigrant's wagon, drawn by a horse escaped from the Apocalypse.

At a jog trot—is that bizarre speed really a jog trot?—we pulled up, the rig, the nag, and I, to the shop where my idol reigned.

Now, at least, I had an excuse for lounging on the sidewalk.

I gave myself the airs of an indifferent coachman, a punctual coachman awaiting his passenger.

It was a busy time. Customers came and went without interruption, carrying their merchandise carefully, so as not to spill the aspic.

She, on her feet, active, always serious, sold the comestibles without a single mistake about the weight or the change.

I was thoroughly charmed by the spectacle, when suddenly I remembered my job as a young coachman.

I turned around. No more wagon! No more dobbin! Flown away, vanished!

Two policemen passed.

I told them my misadventure.

A mob formed immediately. The crowd showed extreme joy at the incident. Street kids, perhaps those I had recently gorged with boar's head and pistachios, taunted me fiercely.

How stupid I must have looked!

But my confusion knew no bounds when I saw, at the door of her shop, my beautiful porkbutcher herself laughing with all the splendor of her pearly teeth.

God, how amused she was!

I never went back to that neighborhood.

ROSETTE

His name was Henri, hers Rose.

But since their first days in love, they had baptized one other Riquet and Rosette.

And it was touching, after their thirty-six years together, to hear them bill and coo like two old pigeons, always tender: my Riquet… my Rosette…

Riquet painted, funny little paintings that were tidy and rococo, apparently soaked in gingerbread juice.

Which did not prevent Rosette from finding her Riquet's paintings admirable:

"How talented you are, my Riquet!"

"And you, my Rosette, how lovely you are!"

Every day, after lunch, Riquet went to take his little stroll on the ramparts.

Rosette saw him to the door, cast a final eye on his toilette, with a flick of her finger removed a speck of dust, adjusted his tie, smoothed down a rebellious cowlick:

"Go, my Riquet, and above all," she added with a menacing finger, "no infidelities!"

And Riquet left, radiant in the triumph of his fine old age, happy and admired.

I liked to visit those old turtledoves, whose comportment made me ashamed of my own young love affairs.

Rosette, still pretty with her black eyes under her silver hair, as rosy as her name, meticulously clean, still almost desirable, at moments, and I told myself that Riquet must have had nothing to complain about, back in the day.

"If you only knew," she used to say to me, "how handsome he was, my Riquet. All of the women got sick just looking at him. But he didn't love anyone but me, and never loved anyone but me."

She remained a few minutes in the silent ecstacy of her memories, and then added, heaving a great sigh:

"I only hope that the Good Lord calls him before me!"

I was profoundly moved by this heroic and simple love.

"Poor Rosette!" I thought. "It won't take her long to follow him into the grave."

One day, I heard that Riquet was dead.

This is how Riquet died:

He was walking in the country.

Out on the sunny and dusty road, a young painter was working on a landscape.

The old artist approached, and could not suppress a start:

"Violet shadows!" he cried.

The young painter, who had not received an extremely meticulous upbringing, replied, without even turning around:

"Would you rather I made them the color of… caca?" (The young artist even pronounced another word.)

Riquet, once challenged, would not admit defeat.

"But after all, monsieur, shadows aren't violet… they're brown!"

The young artist arose, executed a few entrechats in the road, and interrogated Riquet:

"And what about your sister… is she brown?"

Having started in this tone, the discussion soon took a most regrettable esthetic direction.

The young artist called Paul Delaroche a scoundrel, and Riquet claimed that Manet was nothing but a pig.

"But after all," concluded the young artist, "if you don't have a half pound of… caca on each eye, take a look and tell me if those shadows aren't violet?"

For the first time in his old existence, Riquet saw that in fact the shadows of the trees, falling on the road, were inexorably violet.

Poor Riquet received a terrible shock.

He took to bed and never recovered from the emotion.

Eight days later, he died.

My activities in Paris prevented me from attending my old friend's funeral.

I wrote Rosette a good long letter, drawn from the finest part of my heart.

Poor Rosette!

A year later, I received an announcement that was almost like being struck by lightning.

I won't keep you in suspense: Rosette was remarrying.

This time, the thing was worth the trip, and I insisted on seeing this curious ceremony with my own eyes.

Rosette welcomed me cheerfully.

I was cold:

"Congratulations, madame."

"Are you surprised that I would remarry?"

"A bit, madame, may I confess?"

"But why, after all?… A woman my age is not out of the game yet, at fifty-four."

"*Out of the game!* What an expression! If Riquet could hear you…"

"Leave Riquet alone. He's fine where he is."

"And you who asked the Good Lord to call him before you!"

"Well, yes, exactly!" she concluded, with disgusting cynicism.

I, THE UNDERSIGNED

When the Marquis of Puyjuteux died, some three years ago, he left a considerable fortune to his two sons Jacques and Didier.

The two brothers, despite the great sorrow they felt at their loss, bore no resemblance to each other, either physically or morally.

The elder, Jacques, a tubby fellow who was oafish, shortish, boorish, reddish, and unstylish, looked like an overly healthy gentleman-farmer, but a gentleman-farmer who was overwhelmingly farmer and barely gentleman.

Just the opposite, Didier. Tall, thin, wiry, of unparalleled distinction and irresistible charm, Didier could have obtained, for nominal sums, all the grand ladies in the suburbs, and even many of our prettiest coquettes in the Étoile district; but, there you are, Didier was in love with one woman, one little woman, one little woman alone.

Without recalling the features of Cleopatra, the face of Didier's girlfriend—her name was Marie Tournelle—won you over at first sight, for it radiated good humor, good health, goodwill, and, in general, all of the courtesies.

Not for the world would Marie Tournelle have asked a

sou from Didier, which meant that logically, after three years, poor Didier had consumed his share of the inheritance.

One fine morning, as he turned his pockets inside out at his lawyer's office, he realized that he was as peeled as a parsnip, as rinsed as a beer mug, as ruined as a loan shark's clientele.

Marie Tournelle's pretty eyes changed for a few days into graceful fountains, then Didier left Paris and retreated to an old tract of patrimonial land, over there, where he lived by the fruit of his hunting and fishing, plus a small income granted by his brother.

This last, being a practical lad who knew full well he would never be loved for himself, had struck a deal with a young Israelite who was heartless, but strikingly beautiful, named Sarbah Kahn, and paid her a monthly fee to lavish him with her exclusive favors.

The fee was high, but at least Jacques knew what it cost him, and when you know what it costs you (don't forget it), you can spend double or even triple that amount, with still no fear of ruin.

That was how things stood, when Jacques received a letter from poor Didier.

"My dear brother," it said, "in principle, you can do me an extraordinary favor. I'm enormously bored in my tract of patrimonial land, and have a vehement desire to get a little fresh air in Paris. I discovered a usurer, and told him that you were ill, and that I would soon inherit your estate. If you can send me two doctor's certificates, duly signed, you will make yourself worthy of the fine title of brother, etc., etc…"

"I have no objection," murmured Jacques. "But I don't know if I can find two doctors who are crooked enough… Bah! I can always try."

In the house where he lived, there was in fact a highly respected doctor.

Jacques entered his office, and, while visibly clutching a hundred franc note:

"Doctor," he said, "I feel that I'm not long for this world, and to settle certain family matters, I'd like a certificate stating that I'm going to die very soon."

The medical expert examined, palpated, and auscultated Jacques, who had all he could do to keep from laughing, and when it was over:

"Would you like me to write a prescription?" the doctor asked.

"No thank you, doctor, the certificate will be enough."

The scene was repeated exactly with another doctor, this one a member of the Academy of Medicine.

The certificates described terrible lesions on I forget which part of the heart, lesions that gravely jeopardized Jacques's existence.

Never had he laughed so much! A hint of indignation, however, mixed with his hilarity. What crooks, those doctors!

For five louis, you can make them write whatever you want.

And Jacques never stopped his stream of epigrams, invective, and even obscenity about those poor doctors.

One day, however, Jacques consented to stop his stream of epigrams, invective, and even obscenity; it was one day last week, exactly two weeks after his visit to the doctors.

On that day, he died.

The coroner determined that he had succumbed to a disorder provoked by lesions on I forget which part of the heart.

Sarbah Kahn was so upset… But Marie Tournelle was pleased, for her little Didier.

The moral of the story is that when you want a certificate for a serious illness, you should never ask the best doctors, because, you know… those people!

MISTAKE

Mistakes don't count.
LOUIS BRESSON.

It's nice, out in the country, but it was starting to get somewhat boring that year.

And then Suzanne, so funny in Paris, so mischievous, so devil-may-care, decided to take on such airs of respectability, the correct attitude for the lady of the house!

So much for laughs!

Filthy weather, nothing but rain with, now and then, like a coin tossed to a beggar, a poor little ray of pale sunshine.

Ah, it was cheerful!

And the neighbors, besides!

I've seen many neighbors in my life, but never any that stupid, that macabrely goitrous.

So loony, those poor people, that there was always a full moon.

My God! My God! What a summer!

The desire overtook me, rather frequently, to strangle Suzanne, just to have an opportunity to return to Paris, even if it was only in the general area of the penitentiary.

"It's amazing how much fun you seem to have with me!" Suzanne repeated, with a harsh air of angry disappointment.

"Me? I've never laughed so hard!" I regularly replied, unhinging my jaw.

"If I'm not enough for you, invite your friends."

Excellent idea.

I wrote to a few comrades, the best and liveliest ones, letters whose exact tenor I cannot guarantee, but of which this was the gist:

"Dear old thing,

"Be a pal and come spend the day with me on Sunday, and bring your special someone.

"I can't guarantee that you'll have so much fun that you'll lose your mind, but it will be a nice change for me."

Plus a postscript containing information on the most convenient train.

Sunday arrived.

Beginning at dawn, Suzanne was so busy with casseroles and stoves that you would have thought we were expecting a regiment of Pomeranian cavalry.

She had hired, in addition to the little maid we employed daily, several cleaning women from the area, all vigorous, disagreeable, and drunk.

As my friends were expected at 9:22, I left the house at 7 o'clock, for our villa was separated from the station by a distance that measured no less than half a kilometer.

It is useful to add that this half a kilometer was studded with a plethora of taverns, in which each barkeep was my best friend.

Ah, what fine friends those bartenders were, and what trouble they took to fetch, for me, their vermouth-cassis Comète and their bitter-havrais from '64!

Nevertheless, the train arrived.

Young men jumped onto the platform, and also young women.

The young women were the special someones of the young men.

Hello, So-and-So! How are you, Thingummy! How pretty you look, little Whatsit! And you, Etcetera? And you, Etcetera?

In the crowd who arrived to fill my day so racketously, there were two faces I didn't know. We were introduced:

"Our friend Baron Martin, lieutenant in the Spahis."

I bowed; but I already disliked Baron Martin.

"Our little comrade Louise, called Mouillette, one of the glories of the milliners on the rue de la Paix."

I bowed, but I already liked Mouillette to the point of delirium.

The events that transpired that day only confirmed my

first impressions.

Baron Martin, a tall fellow, quite distinguished, with a jaw like a horse, talkative, gesticulatory, demanding attention from everyone, bringing out personal anecdotes on the slightest pretext:

"Something even better happened to me. In Constantine…"

Sometimes, it was in Médéa that something even better happened to him, or else in Tlemcen. Damn!

Young Mouillette, a plump young ashen blonde, not yet twenty, with clear gray eyes, bordered with black eyelashes, eyes that she used to smile, to laugh, and even to guffaw. Do you like young ladies who laugh with their eyes?

I insisted on introducing my guests to my friends among the suburban bartenders, who, I must acknowledge, improvised for the occasion some truly remarkable white wines.

It was much closer to one o'clock than to noon (the appointed time) when we arrived at the house.

Suzanne, in a blue dressing gown, waited at the top of the steps.

She was charming to Baron Martin, and a bit cold to Mouillette.

We sat down to lunch.

Was it the country air, was it the aperitifs? We devoured the food, as if each vermouth had served as an excavator.

Baron Martin, especially, gave his horse's jaw quite a

workout. And I thought, to myself:

"You must not be very happy, you, out in the desert."

Which did not prevent him, besides, from being much friendlier to Suzanne.

Ah, if I had been jealous!

But I could not take my eyes from the sweet Mouillette, she too stuffing herself as if she were deaf, entirely unembarrassed by Suzanne's cool reception.

When we took a walk in the woods, after lunch, I let Baron Martin, Suzanne, and all the other young men and women, go pick rustic bouquets, while I maneuvered, like a torpedo boat, to approach Mouillette.

I had a double objective, to appropriate Mouillette as much for herself as to avenge myself on Baron Martin, for I had no doubt that Mouillette was the girlfriend of the colonial cavalier.

I began the conversation by giving the young woman's buttocks a hearty spank.

I hurt my hand.

"Hey!" said Mouillette.

"All my compliments, mademoiselle."

"For what, monsieur?"

"For the consistency of your bottom."

"What does that mean, consistency?"

"It means that your bottom is pretty damn hard."

"You're not the first to tell me that. At the shop, my friends call me Boxwood Butt."

"And it doesn't bother you?"

"It would bother me more if they called me Library Paste Butt."

Mouillette had wit; I was smitten.

A few minutes after this little chat, I verified, in the darkest corner of the woods, that it was not only her bottom that was like boxwood.

Shouts rang out.

I recognized the voice of my friend Georges, calling "Mouillette! Mouillette!"

"Georges! Georges! Over here!" I called out in turn.

"You're crazy," said Mouillette, "to call Georges."

"No, not at all, Georges will be amused!"

On seeing us, Georges's stupefaction only increased:

"What the hell are you doing, you two?"

"I'll tell you: that filthy swine Baron Martin is flirting with Suzanne, so I had my revenge."

"What do you mean, your revenge?"

"Yes, with mademoiselle."

"But she's my girlfriend, you idiot!"

"Oh, my poor fellow, I'm terribly sorry."

THE VENGEANCE OF D'ESPARBÈS

Clericalism, that is the enemy.
LÉON GAMBETTA

Be assured, O young husband, O Georges, that the d'Esparbès who will be the subject of this story is not the d'Esparbès whom you so advantageously comprise.

The d'Esparbès who will be the subject here is called d'Esparbès in much the same way that I am called Paul de Cassagnac. So, you see!

I only baptized him that because I noticed in him more than one analogical similarity with yourself. For example: he is, like you, not too tall, but well proportioned, as muscular as one could wish, as broad shouldered as nobody else, self-assured. In his brown face, like yours, shine the bright eyes of a child, like yours.

Like you, he was a lance corporal in the light infantry, but unlike you, he did not abandon the alert troops to seek cowardly refuge in the shadow of the flag of the 46th regiment. (Oh, that shadow! Tell me, Georges, tell me, do you remember it?)

There all similarity ends.

You, you are candid, and as talented as the devil. He, he is as tricky as a ball of twine, and a rural postman.

The rest of the story, besides, will open between your two natures imperishable gulfs.

He avenged himself pettily, whereas you, you would have pardoned, as in the Bible, with a prophetic gesture, large and perhaps even circular.

A rural postman, I have proclaimed, and I will not recant.

Georges d'Esparbès—let him keep the name, because it pleases me—brought me my mail every morning.

Every morning, I treated him to a drop of my oldest Calvados, at which I never saw him sneeze. We enjoyed a little chat about the subjects of the day. Often, I accompanied him on the state highways, on the departmental roads, and sometimes on the footpaths.

"THE FOOTPATHS ARE NARROW WAYS," said, not without reason, the late and lamented poet Albert Mérat.

We discussed politics, socialism, religion.

"As for all that," d'Esparbés had announced to me, "me, I'm *electric*."

(I always thought he meant to say *eclectic*.)

And I quickly guessed where his *electricity* came from.

Required by his duties to deliver to the taxpayers the different periodicals that those fine people had paid for, quarterly or annually (according to the length of the subscription), d'Esparbès deducted a small tithe of one gazette a day.

Out of discretion, he changed organs daily.

One day, it was the *Intransigeant*, another day the *Patrie*, the third day the *Chat Noir*, and then the *Univers*, and so on.

This course of reading, quotidian but devoid of homogeneity, had killed, in d'Esparbès's heart, all bias, all conviction, all enthusiasm, and so it was that he had become, in his own forceful term, *electric*.

In this shipwreck of ideas, of splashing debris, floated, O triumph, the radiant buoy of Love, of Love unceasing.

D'Esparbès was in love.

He was in love with a widow, stout, brunette, with little sideburns, already no longer very young, but still as desirable as one could wish.

The desirable widow was not indifferent to the robust shanks—let us say the shanks—of d'Esparbès, and let him know it.

So, the postman's visit to the beautiful widow lasted, perhaps, more time than might seem required to deliver ordinary mail, even were it loaded with grapeshot.

People in the country are not very inquisitive, fortunately.

One day, d'Esparbès delivered my letters and papers, without offering his customary little joke, which was different every time, although without much variation.

His face was upset, his eyes shone maliciously, his mouth was twisted.

"So what's wrong now, my old d'Esparbès?" I asked sympathetically.

"It's… It's… It's nothing!"

Five minutes later, thanks to my skill in questioning others, I knew everything.

What it was, was that the desirable widow was cheating on d'Esparbès, non-stop, and guess with whom?

With Father Chamelle, the vicar of Cornouilly, one of those priests that you cannot comprehend the bishop sending into a respectable parish. A scoundrel, in other words.

D'Esparbès was furious.

"But I'll get my revenge," he concluded. "I'll get my revenge."

D'Esparbès got his revenge, in fact, but he got his revenge in such a way that my pen bridles at the writing of it.

One evening, the humble functionary, after dinner, wandered into one of those little innumerable cabarets on the quais of Houlbec, cabarets frequented by coalmen, dimwitted fishermen, and women who combine the trafficking of their charms with total contempt for the most elementary laws of intimate hygiene.

D'Esparbès spent several minutes with one of these.

Let me add that he got what he wanted.

The following week, the doctor of the administration gave him a week off.

The next Sunday, early in the morning, I was awakened

by d'Esparbès.

I had never seen him so merry.

"Would you like a good laugh?" he asked.

I was affirmative.

"Then hitch up the horses, and let's go to high mass in Cornouilly. You won't waste your time."

We arrived as the faithful were entering the holy place.

Father Chamelle seemed to bring very little verve to his sacred ceremony. Somewhat pale, he mounted the steps to the altar with difficulty.

D'Esparbès was holding his sides.

At the moment when, having presented to his flock the chalice filled with the blood of Christ, the priest was about to swallow the table wine (180 francs a barrel at the station), d'Esparbès arose, and in a piercingly mocking voice, very loud:

"Be careful, father," he cried. "You know very well the doctor told you not to drink it straight!"

FINIS CHAT NOIR!

To Madame Gabrielle Salis

Vixit! to continue proving that one has done one's humanities. Le Chat Noir is dead! Closed, the cabaret! Obliterated, the theater! Comatose, the shadow puppets! Dispersed, the poets and singers! Abolished, the paper!

It is a part of many of us that is going, and when I learned today of the sale of the last paintings, drawings, and other artistic trinkets, which were to be scattered

To the four winds, sir, of the public auctions,

something much like a tear trembled on my aging eyelashes.

Ah, Le Chat Noir, the first Chat Noir, the one on the boulevard Rochechouart!

You are too young, you urchins, to have known that fabulous saloon!

Oh, what nasty kids we were back then, whose only thought was to enrage our poor neighbors!

It was especially a little clockmaker who got the worst of it! We annoyed him so well, or rather so badly, that he soon died of it.

This little clockmaker, whom I hasten first of all to make unsympathetic, by adding that he was as nasty as the mange and frankly usurious in his practices, this little usurer, as I was saying, occupied a cramped little shop, almost a booth, right next to the one where Rodolphe Salis had installed his turbulent cabaret (the first one, of course, the one near l'Elysée-Montmartre).

Soon, with all the artists on the Butte and some from the Latin Quarter crowding into the flanks of Le Chat Noir, the location was clearly becoming too small.

Salis dreamed of expansion, and cast concupiscent looks at the little clockmaker's shop.

"Little clockmaker, my neighbor," the gentleman-cabaretist said to him, "go take your shameful little business elsewhere, and grant me your hovel. For once, you would be worthy of Art and of Montmartre."

But this noble language failed to touch the base soul of the little clockmaker, who was willing to accept the proposition, but only for sums capable of striking terror into the most valorous.

"Ah, so it's like that!" said Salis. "Well then, we shall see!"

And we did see, in fact!

From that moment on, the little clockmaker knew not a single minute of peace.

Only a few months passed before the first manifestations of cerebral disturbance, then senility, and then, finally, his demise.

It would take massive in-quartos to relate in detail the sinister pranks that we strove to invent for our annoying neighbor.

I would like to recount only one, to which our current election gives a hint of topicality.

It was during a time of municipal elections. Paris was flooded with posters and manifestoes (among others, one in which Salis called fiercely for the separation of Montmartre and the State).

One fine evening, at the stroke of midnight, two nice billposters wander into the Chat Noir, armed with a large supply of paper and a full pail of glue.

Immediately, one of our disreputable crowd has the positively brilliant idea of using the posters for the hermetic caulking of the little clockmaker's shop.

And while Salis conscientiously intoxicated the two billposters, we fulfilled their duties with professional care.

In a few minutes, there remained on the front of the shop not a single square centimeter that was not covered with a thick and multiple coating of paper.

As a crowning touch of cruelty, we added to our wheat paste a strong dose of alum, a substance that hardens it and makes it insoluble.

Ah! The next morning, I beg of you to believe that we were not bored!

The little clockmaker literally foamed at the mouth. A sponge in one hand, a scraper in the other, he labored away, shouting a thousand inarticulate blasphemies.

But what could he do?

His store was armored with a terrible substance somewhere between porcelain and rhinoceros hide.

It took him two days before he could free the door and enter his shop.

Those were good times!

NOTES ON THE TEXT

"The Miserable Wretch and the Good Genie" (*Le pauvre bougre et le bon génie*): first published in *Le Chat Noir*, August 1, 1885, then as a monologue by Ollendorff in 1890, with the subtitle "A heartbreaking story sobbed by Coquelin Cadet of the Comédie-Française." In 1899, Allais expanded it into a one-act play; it was performed at the Théâtre des Mathurins, and published by Flammarion. It was also inserted into an odd novel, *Le Boomerang*, in 1903, which was credited to Allais, but ghostwritten by some anonymous and probably needy journalist.

"The late Scribe" was the prolific playwright and librettist Eugène Scribe, who did not write that line.

"Jokes" (*Blagues*): previously unpublished.

Axelsen's watercolor tragedy was told in *Une mort bizarre* ("A Bizarre Death"), which Allais had included in his first book, *A se tordre* (*Double Over,* Black Scat Books: 2016).

Saint-Galmier has been known for its mineral water since Roman times. The water is still marketed, under the brand Badoit.

Jules Lemaître was a theater critic for *Le Journal des Débats*. I am unaware of his role in popularizing the word *gnolle*, which I have rendered here as "chucklehead."

"A Nasty Joke" (*Une mauvaise farce*): *Le Chat Noir*, April 4, 1885, as half of a piece called *Mauvaises blagues* ("Nasty Jokes"). The other half was probably omitted because of its similarity to "Black Christmas": a young man dresses as Pierrot for a ball; when he visits his uncle's factory, hydrogen sulphide turns the lead salts in his makeup black.

"Germs" (*Germes*): previously unpublished.

Charles-Édouard Brown-Séquard was a physiologist, who did a great deal of research on the blood and the nervous system. In his old age, he claimed to have restored his virility with a serum extracted from dog and guinea pig testes. Allais wrote several pieces about this dubious procedure.

"A Historical Footnote" (*Un point d'histoire*): *Le Journal*, December 8, 1892.

At the time, Léon Bourgeois was Secretary of the Interior, and Marie François Sadi Carnot was President.

Caran d'Ache (Emmanuel Poiré) was a cartoonist, considered one of the pioneers of the comic strip. He contributed regularly to *Le Chat Noir*.

"The Futility of Logic" (*Inanité de la logique*): *Le Courrier Français*, September 29, 1885; reprinted in *Le Chat Noir*, September 17, 1887. Allais revised it for this collection.

"The Intermediary" (*L'intermédiaire*): previously unpublished.

Pierre Delcourt contributed to such papers as *La Lanterne, Le Corsaire*, and *La Tribune*. He was director of *Le Chat Noir* in 1887 and 1888.

"Modern Idyll" (*Idylle moderne*): *Le Chat Noir*, June 13, 1885, as *Madrigal manqué* ("Failed Madrigal"), thoroughly rewritten as *Idylle moderne* for *Le Journal*, October 4, 1892.

Friedrich Wilhelm Felix von Bärensprung was a German physician, whose specialties included syphilis and herpes; he was the first to describe *tinea cruris*, now better known as jock itch. The book that Valentine quotes, however (*Investigations in the Natural Science of Men and Animals*), is a massive (13 volumes) work by the Dutch physiologist Jacob Moleschott.

"A Funny Idea" (*Une drôle d'idée*): previously unpublished.

Tirouard-Delatable (de Nuits) sounds uncannily like *tiroir de la table de nuit*: drawer of the nightstand.

"The Good Sentry Rewarded" (*Le bon factionnaire récompensé*): *Le Chat Noir*, December 21, 1889, as *Conte de Noël: Au Poste*. ("Christmas Story: At Headquarters.")

Guy de La Hurlotte appears in a number of Allais's military stories, including "Fancy Dress" and "Aphasia" in *Double Over*.

La broche means "the skewer" and a *baju* is a short Malaysian jacket, but I suspect neither is really significant.

"Bizarroid": previously unpublished.

"Poor Césarine!" (*Pauvre Césarine!*): *Le Chat Noir*, February 19, 1887, as *Pauvre Célina*. Alcide Paquet also had a different name: Zéphyr Lagourde.

It's entirely possible that Césarine's name change was prompted by Jean Richepin's novel of the same name, published in 1888.

There was a blacksmith in Roubaix named Alcide Paquet. He was noted in 1888 for inventing a machine to make horseshoes. This may be purely coincidence.

Aline Leproult baffles me, but Jeanne Beaudon was the real name of Jane Avril, dancer at the Moulin Rouge, who rejected a marriage proposal from Allais.

"Et verbum…": previously unpublished.

"The Henri II Chest" (*Le bahut Henri II*): *Le Chat Noir*, November 26, 1892.

Charles Lavigerie was the archbishop of Carthage and Algiers, and the founder of the White Fathers (who did wear red fezzes). Appropriately, he was an ardent opponent of slavery.

A *saligaud* is a scoundrel.

Timeo Danaos et dona ferentes is a celebrated line from the *Aeneid*: beware of Greeks bearing gifts.

Se non è vero, è ben trovato is a common Italian tag: if it's not true, it's clever.

Rester le bec dans l'eau means to be left in the lurch.

"The Family Trick" (*Le truc de famille*): previously unpublished.

"A New Poet" (*Un poète nouveau*): previously unpublished.

Franc-Nohain (Maurice Legrand) started contributing to *Le Chat Noir* when he was eighteen. He specialized in metrically irregular verse, with forced and slant rhymes, which he called "amorphous poetry." He was a friend of Alfred Jarry, and joined him in puppet shows; Jarry dedicated a chapter of *Exploits and Opinions of Doctor Faustroll, Pataphysician* to him (Chapter 16, "Of the Amorphous Island"). Incidentally, the first king of the island in that chapter has been identified as Allais: he lives on a ladder, and invents a tandem bicycle for quadrupeds. Franc-Nohain's first book, *Inattentions et sollicitudes*, was published in 1894.

"The Dance of the Careless Nephews" appeared in *Le Chat Noir* on August 29, 1891. The uncles in question were Francisque Sarcey and Allais himself. Allais hadn't contributed anything since late June, which meant that

Sarcey had also gone missing.

Allais discreetly omitted the third verse, which goes something like this:

> And so, you understand, we're sick and tired.
> If they went off to sleep with cheap whores, the simps,
> And got their bellies kicked in by the pimps,
> Why should our efforts be required?
> It would certainly be more thorough,
> *To ask at an information bureau.*
> Under the quincunxes,
> We cannot find out uncles.

Hégésippe Moreau was a poet of the early 19th century; he died young, and was considered a tragic and romantic figure. The quatrain attributed to him is indeed his.

"A Petition" (*Une pétition*): *Le Journal*, October 31, 1892.

If Onésime Lahilat has any significance, it eludes me. Onésime is the name of a saint, and "Lahila" appears as a tropical island in Allais's earlier story, "Stopover Romances" (*Amours d'escale*), previously collected in *Long Live Life* (Black Scat Books: 2017).

Pourd-sur-Alaure would be *pour sur, alors*: certainly, then. Haute-Toucque is imaginary, and may refer to the river Touques, not too far from Honfleur.

Marie-François Sadi Carnot was then President; Louis-Mathieu Kornprobst was a lieutenant colonel on Carnot's military staff: in the artillery, that is, not the navy.

"An Autumnal Cliché" (*Un cliché d'arrière-saison*): originally published in *Le Chat Noir*, February 22, 1890, as *Un conseil par semaine* ("Weekly Advice"); revised and expanded for *Le Journal*, November 2, 1892, under the title *Qu'est-ce que ça peut bien nous faire que Paris rentre.—Une volumineuse correspondance.—Un bon conseil.—Un jour chic à cent sous.* ("What do we care if Paris returns.—Voluminous correspondence.—Good advice.—An exclusive day for a hundred sous.")

"A New Organ" (*Un nouvel organe*): previously unpublished.

Josephin Péladan had declared himself an Abyssinian "Sâr," and founded a quixotic Rosicrucian-Catholic-Wagnerian order, remembered today for the salons it presented in the late 1890s. He was widely ridiculed by Allais and his circle; his questionable hygiene was a running joke.

The three Coquelins—Constant, his son Jean, and his brother Ernest—often performed together. Ernest, known as Coquelin Cadet (the younger Coquelin), specialized in comic monologues, and performed several by Allais.

Paul Delair was a playwright, poet, and singer.

Tristan Bernard and Pierre Veber were both playwrights and humorists; Bernard wrote a one-act play with Allais, *Silvérie*. The three were close: in 1893, they all lived on rue

Édouard-Detaille, Bernard at number 9, Veber (who had married Bernard's sister) and Allais and his wife at number 7.

"Han Rybeck, or The Stirrup Cup: An Icelandic Story" (*Han Rybeck ou le coup de l'étrier: conte islandais*): *Le Journal*, October 24, 1892.

It helps to know that this is a parody of Pierre Loti's 1886 novel *Pecheur d'Islande* (*An Iceland Fisherman*). It may also help to know that Allais is much bawdier than Loti.

All of the names are puns, usually on Allais's colleagues.

Han Rybeck is Henri Becque, a playwright best known now for initiating the "theater of cruelty." Loti's fisherman was Yann Gaos.

Polalek VI is Paul Alexis, a playwright, novelist, and journalist. He was a friend of Zola, and active in the naturalist movement. He was also a regular contributor to *Le Journal*.

Lagrenn-Houyer is *La Grenouillère* (The Frogpond), then a floating restaurant in Paris.

Paule Norr is *Pôle Nord* (North Pole).

Fern Anxo is Fernand Xau, the editor of *Le Journal*.

"A News Item" (*Un fait-divers*): *Le Journal*, October 15, 1892, under the title *Préambule oiseux.—Intelligence des bêtes.—Encore des cambrioleurs!—Un chien mêlé.—Voleurs volés*. ("Idle preamble.—Intelligence of animals.—Burglars again!—A mutt.—Thieves flown.") The original had this "idle preamble":

What I am about to recount, good people, belongs in the domain of the news item, much more than in any other rubric. Why then did this story not appear under the signature of my excellent colleague *le Quart d'Oeil* (*de Rabelais?*). I will consent to tell you, although my contract with the *Journal* does not require any explanations to the public.

This story, or rather this simple news item—because, I repeat, it is a simple news item—this simple news item, as I was saying, appears under a special rubric, because, considered as a little column, I will be paid an insane price for it, whereas it would have brought me only a pitiful sum otherwise.

Without being thirsty for lucre, I do not spit on gold, united as I am to a young companion who is charming, but costly.

Let us stop this useless preamble and get to the facts.

Le Vieux Caporal was a play by Philippe Dumanoir and Adolphe d'Ennay, first performed in 1856.

"Castor" means "beaver"; for some reason, it's a popular name for dogs.

The Tempest lantern is my substitution for the original Levent lantern; *le vent* means wind, thus provoking Allais's aside.

And in the preamble, Quart d'Oeil was the signature attached to a column of short news items, mostly about crime. A *quart d'oeil* is a police officer; Allais puns on *quart d'heure*, quarter hour. And "Rabelais's quarter hour" is the time to pay the bill.

"Even" (*Quittes*): previously unpublished. Allais later revised it for *Captain Cap* (Black Scat Books: 2013).

Captain Cap was a real person, Albert Caperon, a genial barfly whom Allais turned into a world adventurer. He was born in France, but raised in California; Allais apparently thought he was Canadian because he was a member of the Gardenia club, which included many Québecois.

The Corrèze is a river in southwestern France, unsuitable for whaling.

There is a Mont Mulot in Calvados, not far from Honfleur; this may be what Allais has in mind. However, Montmulot (Mount Mouse) may also be a pun on Montmartre (Mount Marten).

"The Meat-Land": *Le Journal*, October 22, 1892. Reprinted in *Le Chat Noir*, April 1, 1893. Allais also revised this one for *Captain Cap.*

The people of Gascony are traditionally known as braggarts.

Paul Fabre was the son and secretary of Hector Fabre, the General Agent for Canada in Paris. He (the son) later became the editor of Paris-Canada.

Maurice O'Reilly was born in Rouen, but had lived in Canada. He contributed to *Le Chat Noir*, and made a memorable trip to England in 1890 with Allais and George Auriol. He and Paul Fabre directed the Gardenia club, favored by Canadians, where Allais first met Cap.

"Arfled": *Le Chat Noir*, May 28, 1887.

The Three-Hemispheres Hotel was based on The Two-Hemispheres Hotel, on the rue des Martyrs, where Allais did, in fact, live at the time.

Pioncer means "to sleep"; we can assume that M. Pionce was the drowsy type.

"The Forgotten Pipe" (*La pipe oubliée*): previously unpublished.

Claude Chappe invented a relay semaphore system that was used from 1792 to 1852, when it was made obsolete by the telegraph.

"A White Night for a Red Hussar" (*La nuit blanche d'un hussard rouge*): first published in *Le Chat Noir*, January 8, 1887, then reprinted later that year by Ollendorff.

"Black Christmas": *Le Chat Noir*, December 27, 1890, as *Conte de Noël* ("Christmas Story").

Saadi, or Abū-Muhammad Muṣliḥ al-Dīn bin Abdallāh Shīrāzī, was a renowned Persian poet of the 13th century, a time and place innocent of tobacco.

S. Cargo is reminiscent of an *escargot* (snail).

Patrice de Mac Mahon was President of France from 1873 to 1879. A probably apocryphal story has him visiting a school, and being introduced to an African student. "You're the Negro?" he asked. "Well then, continue!"

Edmond Blanc was a politician and horse breeder; his name, of course, means "white."

"One for Tomorrow" (*Une de demain*): previously unpublished.

"A Luminous Idea" (*Une idée lumineuse*): first published in *Le Chat Noir*, November 19, 1887, as *Un inventeur* ("An inventor"), and then reissued under its new title by Ollendorff in 1888, with the subtitle "Monologue performed by Coquelin Cadet of the Comédie-Française."

General Ernest Boulanger was a populist politician, a strange mixture of progressive and proto-fascist.

Francisque Sarcey, as noted previously, was a theater critic, and one of Allais's favorite targets. His obesity is the pertinent characteristic here.

Sarah Bernhardt was not only renowned as an actress, but esteemed by bohemians as an honorary member of the Hydropathes.

"Suggestion": previously unpublished. Allais later revised it for *Captain Cap*.

"Absinthes": *Le Chat Noir*, July 25, 1885.
La Grande Marnière was a novel by Georges Ohnet, published in 1885.
Anatole Beaucanard is a fictional nonentity; *beau canard* means "beautiful duck."
Édouard Dujardin's 1887 novella *Les lauriers sont coupés* is often cited as the first example of the interior monologue, and Joyce himself claimed it as an inspiration. Allais's story was published two years earlier.

"The Parrot" (*Le perroquet*): *Le Journal*, September 29, 1892. This was Allais's first piece for *Le Journal*.
En r'venant de Suresnes, with lyrics by Émile Joinneau and Horace Delattre, and music by Émile Spencer, was published in 1883. It was not Brazilian.

"Forgetfulness" (*Étourderie*): *Le Courrier Français*, February 14, 1886, as *L'étourdie* ("The Forgetful Woman"), reprinted in *Le Chat Noir*, March 5, 1887 and *Gil Blas illustré*,

August 23, 1891 (as *Étourderie*).

The Théâtre de la Porte-Saint-Martin was founded in 1781, and is still running. Paul Lordon was indeed secretary; he also wrote for the *Écho de Paris*, and was a member of the Hydropathes.

"An Unfortunate" (*Un malheureux*): *Le Journal*, January 22, 1893, as *Noble mission.—Une sale époque.—Lettre d'un désespéré.—Une tournée fructueuse.—Appel suprême.* ("Noble mission.—A filthy era.—Letter from a desperate man.—A fruitful tour.—Last call.")

"A Will" (*Un testament*): previously unpublished.

Our landowner's womanizing is of Biblical proportions, apparently recalling Nimrod, who was a mighty hunter before the Lord (Genesis 10:9).

"Love Among Syrian Tortoises" (*L'amour chez les tortues syriaques*): *Le Journal*, November 6, 1892.

In addition to his columns for *Le Temps*, Gaspard de Cherville wrote books on hunting and country life, and collaborated on several novels with Alexandre Dumas.

Adrien Hébrard was indeed the director of *Le Temps*.

The young and handsome Dunois is a crusader in the song *Partant pour la Syrie* ("Leaving for Syria") by Alexandre de Laborde and Hortense de Beauharnais, from 1807.

"The Gentleman and the Hardware Clerk: An English Story" (*Le monsieur et le quincaillier: histoire anglaise*): *Le Journal*, February 10, 1893.

"A Good Society" (*Une Bonne Oeuvre*): *Le Journal*, December 21, 1892, as *Une oeuvre intéressante.—Juste hommage à l'auteur.—Cinquante-quatre mille kilogrammes de bois perdu journellement.—Emotion bien compréhensible.— Appel à la charité.* ("An interesting society.—Fitting homage to the author.—Fifty-four thousand kilograms of wood lost every day.— Quite understandable emotion.—Appeal to charity.")

Pas tant de rouspétance means "not so much grumbling."

The Panama scandal dominated the news in 1892: the Panama Canal Company went bankrupt, losing money for thousands of investors; hundreds of politicians accepted bribes to cover up their corruption and incompetence.

"The Cyclist" (*Le cycliste*): previously unpublished.

EXTRA STORIES

"The Beautiful Porkbutcher" (*La belle charcutière*): *Le Courrier Français*, March 21, 1886.

"Rosette": *Le Chat Noir*, March 24, 1888.

Paul Delaroche was known for his meticulously realistic historical paintings.

"I, the Undersigned" (*Je, soussigné*): *Le Chat Noir*, March 23, 1889.

Puyjuteux is "Mount Juicy"; *depuis juteux* is "since juicy," or "since profitable."

Ma ritournelle is "my song"; *sarbacane* is "blowpipe."

"Mistake" (*Erreur*): *Le Chat Noir*, December 14, 1889.

Louis-Antoine-Maurice Bresson was a celebrated architect; the tag, however, is traditional.

The Spahis were the French cavalry stationed in Algeria.

A *mouillette* is a strip of bread, usually dipped into a boiled egg.

"The Vengeance of d'Esparbès" (*La vengeance de d'Esparbès*): *Le Chat Noir*, October 17, 1891.

Georges d'Esparbès was a novelist, poet, and playwright; he was a member of the Barbus, and a regular at the Chat Noir. He specialised in stories about military life. In 1887, Allais served under him in the 46th regiment, in Paris.

Léon Gambetta was a French politician; the epigraph is genuine.

Paul de Cassagnac (or, to grant him his full name,

Paul Adolphe Marie Prosper Granier de Cassagnac) was a journalist and politician, known for his radically conservative, Bonapartist views.

Albert Mérat was a poet; that line is his.

L'abbé Chamelle is named after that French staple *la béchamel* (white sauce).

Cornouilly seems to be a combination of *corniaud* (idiot) and Nouilly (a commune in the Moselle department).

"Finis Chat Noir!": *Le Journal*, May 17, 1898.

I can't trace that line of verse. It may be due to Allais himself, who occasionally liked to burst into alexandrines.

ABOUT THE TRANSLATOR

Doug Skinner has contributed articles, cartoons, and fiction to *Black Scat Review, Oulipo Pornobongo, The Fortean Times, Strange Attractor Journal, Fate, Weirdo, The Anomalist, Nickelodeon, Cabinet*, and other fine publications. Black Scat has published several collections of his stories and cartoons, as well as his translations of Alphonse Allais, Isidore Isou, and other avant-garde luminaries.

He has written music for several dance companies, including ODC-San Francisco and Margaret Jenkins; his scores for actor/clown Bill Irwin include *The Regard of Flight, The Courtroom, The Regard Evening*, and *The Harlequin Studies*. He has performed his songs in many theaters, clubs, and cabarets. His puppet shows with Michael Smith have been seen everywhere from Caroline's Comedy Club in Manhattan to the Museum of Contemporary Art in Los Angeles.

TV and movie appearances include *Great Performances, The '90s, Martin Mull's Talent Takes a Holiday, Ed, Crocodile Dundee II*, and a smattering of commercials.

He lived for decades in Manhattan, but has moved to New Paltz, a few miles to the north.

The Alphonse Allais Collection
Published by Black Scat Books

"... one of the great masterpieces of humorous literature."

—*nooSFere Littérature*

"...apart from being long-awaited, *Captain Cap* also comes at a timely moment because its ironies are particularly apposite today as we witness global intellectual colonization." — *Leonardo Reviews*

Translated and with an introduction, notes, and illustrations by Doug Skinner, this is the complete, unabridged text of the original 1902 French classic by the peerless humorist, Alphonse Allais. This deluxe edition also features eight uncollected "Captain Cap" stories, plus a "Cappendix" of rare historical pictures. Over 360 pages of absurdist mirth and howls of laughter.

This collection of Allais's rare theatrical texts includes original translations—never before published in English—of ten monologues, three one-act plays, and twelve shorter dialogues, skits and burlesques drawn from his columns in such publications as **Le Chat Noir** and **L'Hydropathe**. This delightful compilation by Doug Skinner (with fascinating notes on the texts) is proto-Dada at its most delicious.

"No Oulipian could fail to be enchanted by his essentially ironic tales, in which he juggles the rhetorical and narrative components of writing with rigorous logic and inexhaustibly zany results." —Harry Mathews

"Allais comes across as a very modern writer, and his work as an experimental enterprise which is exemplary in many ways... it is also quite possible to invoke such writers as Queneau, Calvino, and Borges." —Jean-Marie Defays

Belly laughs guaranteed!

Here is the master absurdist's inaugural collection, containing his hand-picked favorites from the pages of Le Chat Noir, the bohemian journal that amused and scandalized Paris. Here you'll find Allais in the first flush of his comic genius, spinning out elegant and hilarious gems of black humor on suicide, murder, obsession, and adultery. You will meet the philosophical cuckold, the young lady in love with a pig, the inventor of the Tumultoscope, and Ferdinand, the most resourceful duck in literature. Among the highlights is Allais's most famous story, "A Thoroughly Parisian Drama," a favorite of André Breton and Umberto Eco. This is the book's first publication in English, and features seven additional stories from **Le Chat Noir**, as well as a sublime introduction, notes on the text, and drawings by Doug Skinner.

Alphonse Allais's elegance, scientific curiosity, preoccupation with language and logic, wordplay and flashes of cruelty inspired Alfred Jarry, as well as succeeding generations of Surrealists, Pataphysicians, and Oulipians. **The Squadron's Umbrella** collects 39 of his funniest stories — many originally published in the legendary paper **Le Chat Noir**, written for the Bohemians of Montmartre. Included are such classic pranks on the reader as "The Templars" (in which the plot becomes secondary to remembering the hero's name) and "Like the Others" (in which a lover's attempts to emulate his rivals lead to fatal but inevitable results.).

As the author promises, this book contains no umbrella and the subject of squadrons is "not even broached."

"... effervescent and flavorful, perfect in its way."
— *Wuthering Expectations*

Adapted to film four times, **L'Affaire Blaireau** has remained popular and in print in France since its original appearance in 1899. This is its first publication in English. It is humorist Alphonse Allais's only novel and, in the words of translator Doug Skinner: "It isn't quite as wild or cruel as his early stories, but I find it delicious anyway. Summer in the provinces, the shrewd but impressionable Blaireau, futile political squabbles, a ridiculous but charming love story, what more could one want? And innocence is rewarded!" Indeed, this novel is a rare find to be savored by the author's growing circle of fans in America

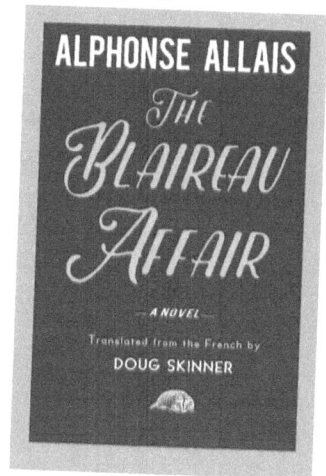

"...the unexpected is suddenly present, and there is rudeness, as well as a savagery of attack that we simply can't imagine anyone doing to any well-known columnist of today and getting away with it."

— Jeff Bursey

Alphonse Allais transforms the conservative French drama critic Francisque Sarcey into an Ubuesque piñata in a series of columns published under Sarcey's name, in the newspaper **Le Chat Noir**. The pseudo-Sarcey becomes a prattling idiot, bragging about his appetite and complaining about his impotence, a memorable comic character who often eclipsed the original. This sustained journalistic prank — compiled and translated by Doug Skinner — is a classic of black humor.

"Absurdism in all its glory....Anyone who wants to learn invaluable information about Sarcey's love for young women, the weather at the end of the 19th century (which seems surprisingly similar to that of today), his love of food (and doubtful vegetarianism) or his beloved umbrella, is highly advised to read I Am Sarcey." —Edith Doove

Visit BlackScatBooks.net

VIVE LA VIE! — stories from the pages of LE CHAT NOIR, packed with madcap (and bawdy) tales of love, adultery, the supernatural, military life, and FAKE NEWS. These texts are quintessentially Allaisian, spiked with absurd digressions, parenthetical asides, footnotes, puns, jokes, military jargon, Parisian slang, neologisms, dog Latin, literary quotations, and other unmentionable forms of wordplay. This special Black Scat edition features four additional short stories not included in the original French volume, as well as a lively introduction, illustrations, and fascinating notes on the text by Doug Skinner. Explosions of laughter guaranteed.

This full-color illustrated volume unmasks a quintessential Allaisian tale — a pataphysical text admired by André Breton and included in his seminal "Anthologie de l'humour noir." It was celebrated by the French group Oulipo, and has been the subject of scholarly studies by the writer and semiotician Umberto Eco, Francis Corblin, and others. Originally published under the title "Un drame bien parisien," this Black Scat chapbook edition has been adapted and illustrated by artist Norman Conquest, and includes an introduction and notes on the text by Doug Skinner.

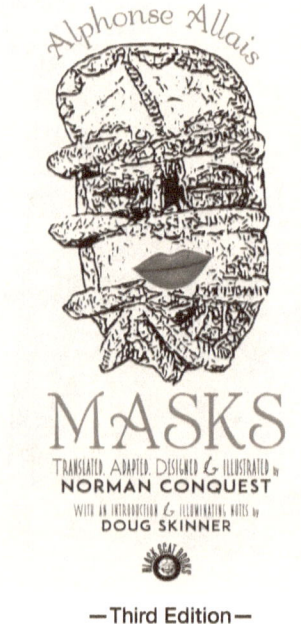

MASKS

TRANSLATED, ADAPTED, DESIGNED & ILLUSTRATED by
NORMAN CONQUEST
WITH AN INTRODUCTION & ILLUMINATING NOTES by
DOUG SKINNER

—Third Edition—

www.ingramcontent.com/pod-product-compliance
Lightning Source LLC
Chambersburg PA
CBHW031409250626
47155CB00004B/1473